I AL●NE

A.J. BRITT

ALONE

BOOK ONE

The thick falling snow blurs the distant pasture with a white haze. Other than the crosshairs in my scope, all else remains foggy. I sit still under a pile of decaying leaves, which keeps me warm and hidden.

The barrel protrudes out of the leaves, mimicking a dead stick. Despite its metallic sheen, it blends in well. Cold and lifeless like its surroundings. Fallen snow gathers at the end of the .308 Remington sniper rifle, a welcomed addition to its camouflage.

Not long ago, they considered this rifle a piece of junk. Another relic for the recycle pile. Now, it's the most valuable rifle on the planet. It's undetectable. A pre-GRID rifle. A pre-war rifle. My lifeline. My world. I know this gun better than I know my own breathing, and if it weren't for one, I wouldn't have the other. When it's in my hands, I feel safe. I feel secure. It's a craftsmanship of confidence, and it's the last of its kind.

Hunting while being hunted is no easy task. With Eaters and Red Empire patrols on the prowl, I must maintain patience. The ability to sit still for hours and take in my surroundings is a discipline I mastered during the war.

I turn my head, allowing my eyes a panoramic view of the pasture. Loud noises will give my position away. Especially an echoing rifle blast. Double-checking everything out here is crucial, but I've already done my reconnaissance. Twice. So, I know it's safe.

Wait! Movement...

I scan the area where I saw the movement. Please don't let it be an Eater!

Then, I spot an elk cow passing through the branches of a hemlock tree. A pile of snow falls off the limbs and lands on her back. I can barely make her out in my scope as I line her up in the crosshairs, but from what I can tell, she's a beautiful elk. Her death will be my lifesaver. My heart races in anticipation. Despite the freezing cold, my toes that are sticking out of my raggedy socks begin to sweat within my boots. It reminds me of why I need this meat—a nice pair of wool socks for a rack of elk ribs would be nice.

The rush of adrenaline coursing through me doesn't waver my focus. I stay calm because this is what I was trained to do. Killer, hunter, sniper—all titles given to me that fit perfectly. The Marines called me a sniper, the villagers call me a hunter, and the Red Empire calls me a killer. All are right.

With only a few bullets to spare, I never hurry my shots. Judging the wind strength, I dial in the scope for a 500-yard shot. It's got to be the exact trajectory, so I double-check the wind speed again. If I miss, the echoing shot will cause her to dart back into the woods.

My finger caresses the metal trigger. Back and forth, back and forth, keeping my trigger finger extra sensitive. It's also a bad habit I picked up. I know how much pressure it takes for the firing pin to be released when I pull the trigger.

Halfway through exhaling, I stop and hold the remaining air inside my lungs. Calmness falls over me like a blanket. *Thump-thump. Thump--thump. Thump---thump.* I can feel the tempo of my heart slowing. Should I put too much pressure on the gun or twitch even slightly, the shot will veer off target. One millimeter of involuntary movement and it could end up two yards away from where I want it to go. I brace my left hand under the foregrip of the rifle, allowing me to secure it from moving when the pin strikes the primer. I start to pull the trigger but stop.

The elk turns to go back into the woods, and I see her condition. Her cheek meat is hanging off her face, and her molars are exposed. Broken ribs protrude from her side, and blood drips from her mangled skin. The snow that falls on her changes color instantly from white to a rosy tinge. Her hind leg is missing, and a continuous stream of red liquid runs from the nub. She attempts to clean her wounds, but each time she tries, she ends up collapsing onto the ground. From the amount of blood loss, it appears she no longer has the strength to move again. I want to end her pain, but I must conserve my bullets as a means of survival.

I have one in the chamber, four in the box magazine, and ten in my pocket; fifteen total. If I die tomorrow, fifteen is plenty. If I live another year, it's not enough. Although I desperately wish to save her from suffering, at this moment I need to save myself.

2

Escaping the Eaters couldn't have been easy. They had sunk their teeth into her and attempted to tear her apart, yet something inside gave her the strength to carry on. Eaters swarm fast, driven by sheer hunger rather than any kind of skill.

Once they sink their teeth into something, the decaying process begins immediately. A putrid scent comes off the wound, attracting more of them like moths to a flame. It's instinctual for them—like a bee finding a flower or a shark sensing blood in the water. They are drawn to the rotting flesh, and when they find it, they devour it without mercy.

I can't stay here any longer. That elk is a walking dinner bell. At least this morning was more eventful than usual. I stand from the pile of leaves that have been hiding me, wincing as my muscles protest the sudden movement after hours of stillness. I slowly stretch out my back and thighs, trying to ease some of the ache. The blood rushes to my head, and the cold doesn't help with the stiffness.

I wipe my hands back and forth across my body to brush off the clinging snowflakes, sticks, and dead leaves. The cold air immediately takes away any warmth I had. I bend over and heave up my heavy backpack, filled with meat from an elk I had shot and killed three days prior. Luck was on my side—there is no rotten flesh beacon or all-you-can-eat buffet stuffed in this bag: just good wholesome meat for trade.

Most survivors migrate toward abandoned log cabins or outpost buildings in these mountains. They become homesteaders, and as they do, more arrive looking for a place to stay. With no access to electricity or plumbing, they form settlements and rely on one another for basic needs and resources. Sharing skills is important for survival; it's what keeps these little villages alive.

For me though, I'm what you call a loner. I keep company with lonely. It's just too painful having friends. One day you're laughing at a buddy's joke, and the next day you're rummaging through his stuff to see if he left anything useful behind because he's dead.

The villagers and I share a mutual understanding that we can't trust anyone. We stay away from the abandoned cities, where Eaters had migrated to in the early days of the war. Corpses piled up in the city streets, and the Eaters feasted on them until there was nothing left. When the dead bodies ran out, they started hunting the living, which is why people moved to the mountains.

The Red Empire remained in the abandoned cities. Their mission seemed to be focused on wiping us out, but that has since changed; now they seem more interested in disposing of Eaters. I'm sure they find it difficult to settle with so many of them wandering about.

I saw a village about half a day's journey from here. I scouted it for a whole day, and they seemed like a bunch of busy bees. They never even noticed I was watching them.

I assume they were civilian survivors, but I had no way of knowing for sure. All I knew was that I have not seen any hunters while I was observing them, so the villagers must have been growing spices, vegetables, and fruits during the summertime. That means my meat should be worth double what I usually get if I sell it there.

Villages like these are better than ex-military villages. Ex-military villages are full of hunters and testosterone-driven decision-makers that do not need what I offer.

There are some other settlements in the mountains, like the Loco Solos. They rely on Eaters for their food, and I don't know the medical implications of ingesting them—I assume that if you cook them and avoid their saliva, you're safe. From observing the Loco Solos, eating Eaters makes you delusional and aggressive: short-tempered and unable to form complete sentences. They always seem to be mad at themselves. I watched one punch himself so hard he nearly knocked himself unconscious. After he had spat out a tooth, he started laughing and bumbling as if to congratulate himself on his victory. The Loco Solos consider Eaters a type of livestock, and even from as far away as a football field I can smell the putrid stench of their villages. Just thinking about it makes my eyes water. I've since learned to stay far away from them.

On my hike to the village, I can feel my eyelids getting heavy. I've been awake too long. I need to rest before I lose my edge. The eyes see things that aren't there when you're too tired. Thirty yards off the trail, I see a fallen white ash tree that looks like a good spot to take a break. Before I settle in, I take my bag of meat and bury it under some loose slate rocks and dead leaves fifty yards away. I would tie it up in a tree, but I'm too exhausted. Feeling confident about the hiding spot, I walk back to the white ash tree. I wedge myself into the crevice of the trunk and the ground. Half of me is hidden, but the other half sticks out. I pull as many leaves and sticks as possible on top of my exposed parts for camouflage. Keeping my food away from me gives me an advantage if an Eater or bear detects its smell. Even though bears are just folklore nowadays, I keep watch anyway.

I slip in and out of sleep, the crisp scent of pine in the air stirring me awake. It brings me back to that special Christmas when my dad brought a giant tree into our little house, its branches brushing against the walls as he dragged it through the doorway. His smile wide and his voice booming, he said, "A tree needs to be big, son! The bigger the tree, the greater the Christmas spirit."

He hoisted the tree, angling it down into the stand. A strong pine smell rose from the freshly cut bottom. He attempted to straighten it up, but its top scraped our ceiling and made a hole in it. Dad glanced nervously toward the kitchen, where Mom was baking cookies. In a panic, he attempted to pull the tree back down, only succeeding in getting it wedged in place. I could almost hear my mom's voice in my head, saying: *Sweetheart, this tree is too big for our house.*

Dad worked frantically to dislodge the tree from the ceiling, muttering for me to get drywall putty from the garage before Mom saw. I started in that direction, but not before giving Dad's efforts one last amused look. Suddenly, a large sheet of drywall fell from above onto his head. The room clouded over with white powder, and Mom emerged from the kitchen. Dad's dark hair was now completely covered in white, matching all the living room furniture. Mom didn't even flinch.

"I told you it was too big for the house." She turned and went back into the kitchen without saying another word. I heard her laughing. Dad looked at me and smiled.

"You see Drift, it's a white Christmas after all. The bigger the tree, the greater the Christmas spirit."

I start to doze off, comforted by the memories flashing through my mind. After thirty minutes, I'm startled awake by the distant barking of a dog. Not wanting to make sudden movements in case the canine is nearby with its human companion, I stay hidden and peek out from under the tree trunk. Another bark reverberates in the distance. The echo is far away. I'm at a safe distance. Sliding out from the tree, I look over the trunk, exposing as little of my head as possible. Scanning the trail till I'm satisfied no one is around, I stand up. I retrieve the bag of meat, strapping it on my back again. It fits the same way it came off: heavy and tight.

As I head back to the trail, I hear the distinct rustling of leaves and stop walking. My hearts beating wildly as I scan for any sign of the barking dog. But it's not a dog; it's something much more sinister. A low rumble catches my attention, and when I turn in its direction, I see an approaching wave of brown leaves. Inches away, I make out the shape of a T8. Dread courses through me—this is why Eaters became Eaters—the Red Empire had unleashed this weapon during the war, and it had wreaked unimaginable havoc on those exposed to the chemicals that spew out of it. It did its job so well and continued to do it even after the war. The metallic tick is tear shaped. Its body and thin eight legs make it seem more alien like than robotic. Its revolute legs run to sharp points that dig into the ground.

My backpack hits the ground with a thud. I drop it to lose the weight. My feet slam against the dirt as I take off, running as fast as I can in desperation to outrun the T8 robot. I slide along the dirt, memories of sliding into second base come back to me. Adrenaline pulsing in my veins, I flip onto my stomach and pull my rifle off my shoulder, taking aim. A chill runs down my spine. Thermal imaging and GPS pin drops keeps these things on the trail of their prey—me!

My knuckles turning white as I lie flat on my stomach. Carefully, I slide my elbow onto the ground and position the butt of the gun up to my shoulder. With a deep breath, I pull back and thrust the deadbolt forward causing a loud click, sending a .308 caliber bullet into the chamber. Just fifteen bullets and fifteen seconds—that is all I have. My food was supposed to come from this round, but if I'm dead, what good will that do me? My heart pounds wildly as I start rubbing the trigger. With laser focus on the T8, I hold my breath. The T8 rises to its hind leg. Ready to spew out its gas. To keep themselves safe, they usually leave twenty yards of space between them and their victims. But alongside the gas comes an acidic liquid. I know what it does to human flesh. It turns it into a jelly-like gooey mess in seconds. Thank God for those twenty yards.

My finger curls around the trigger as my palm sweats anxiously. I peer through the scope, my vision locked on the metal tic's belly, where a single red dot appears. The red dot is no larger than a pencil eraser, and yet it is my only hope of killing this thing. I've tried to kill them a million different ways, but this is the only successful one I've found. It dares me to hit the sweet spot. I exhale slowly, aligning the crosshairs until the dot lies in its center.

One thousand one. One thousand two.

Lucky for me, once they are on their hind legs, they don't move anymore. It takes fifteen seconds for the two liquids inside them to merge with each other and become the poisonous gas. I've gotten T8s on their first seconds, and I've gotten them in their fourteenth second. Some I've missed entirely.

One thousand six. One thousand seven.

I pull my finger back on the trigger with one fluid motion. *Peeuwooooo.* When I shoot an intense heat flashes my face. It's a direct hit. I close my eyes because it's so bright. Even with them shut, I can see red orbs chasing each other behind my eyelids. Kind of like the phosphorus bombs used on HUV tanks during the war.

Eight seconds seems to be my average these days. Standing up, I wipe away the clinging leaves. I must be immune to the gas at this point. I haven't changed into an Eater, and I've walked through many T8 clouds during the war, but it's the GPS pin drop giving my location away that scares me the most. Also, I'd hate for someone down the trail who isn't immune to get sprayed by a T8. We don't need any more Eaters around here. It's worth the bullet.

With a swift movement, I snatch the empty brass casing as it is ejected from my gun. My pouch holds twelve other spent bullet casings. I save them just in case I come across gunpowder and lead out here. Reaching into my pocket, I take out a rag and tightly wrap the spent bullet. The fabric keeps them from making any noise when I'm moving, which is essential, since any sound of clanging brass can easily get me killed. Silence keeps me alive.

I walk over to investigate the T8. Some people collect the little solar panels on their backs, but this one disintegrated in the explosion. They rarely survive the blast, but sometimes I get lucky. After making sure the fire is completely extinguished by stomping on the burning leaves, I kick what's left of the T-8 off the path so it is out of sight and out of mind for anyone who passes by later. Not many people are able to take down these things successfully, so I do not want to leave any evidence behind.

Hoisting my backpack back onto my shoulders, I start back down the trail. Hopefully no one heard the rifle or witnessed the explosion of the T8.

I notice a brick-and-mortar building a little off the trail. It's surrounded by brown, dormant weeds sticking out of freshly fallen snow. Leafless vines cling to the bricks. I'm convinced they are the reason the building is standing at all. Keeping cautious and alert, I walk to the building. There could be something worth trading in here. Maybe bullets. Maybe batteries. Hell, maybe just a place to sleep when the weather sucks. The trail that leads to the door is made of gravel. The snow is not sticking to it because the sun is heating the rocks. I know I should walk around the building first. Scout for footprints or other signs. For some reason I don't. It's so quiet.

The metal frame that once held the glass door in place is bent and rusted. Shards of broken glass glint in the sunshine, scattered around the threshold. It's obvious this place was ransacked a long time ago. All that's left is the skeletal remains of an office chair, a gray file cabinet with one side caved in and its drawers strewn about the floor, and a warped, discolored wooden desk that looks more like potential firewood than a desk.

The letters on the wall behind the desk hang precariously, a hodgepodge of rusty metal, peeling paint, and bolts. The N-O-R hangs crookedly with some space next to it, followed by a tarnished

C. More gaps between letters and then R-O-L, a testament of the sign's age and neglect. One last missing letter before N-A with a space between L-U-M-B. I stare at it for a minute, trying to make sense of the remnants. The possibilities swirl in my mind until I settle on North Carolina Lumber. The sign may be faded, but its history is still etched into every dusty crevice and cranny.

Dark wood panels cover the walls. Some hang on to the wall for dear life, and others have given up and rest on the ground. Most of them are gnarled, contorted by temperature change and water damage, their glossy finish having dulled to a matte sheen.

Cold wind blows across the threshold as I step farther into the poorly lit room, a hint of jasmine drifting through the air. Its presence is perplexing; such a sweet fragrance feels out of place among the musty mildew and pungent urine. With each step I take, my boot sinks deep into the soggy fibers, leaving behind an imprint. As I scan my surroundings, my gaze is drawn to a set of shallow footprints near the far wall. They are small, delicate—barely making an imprint in the soggy carpet.

At the rear of the room, there is a shut door. Whoever made the footprints had walked through it as if it were not there. Closed doors scare the hell out of me; they can hold valuable items or something more sinister. But the fresh tracks and this strange place give me a reason to be cautious. Should I investigate, or is it better to just walk away? Whoever made these footprints could track me down if I just walk away. Kill me and take everything I have. No. I have to see what is on the other side.

I reach for the door handle, but it won't move. I twist and tug on it, and then I give the door a hard shove with my shoulder. But still nothing happens. If there's someone behind this door, they know I'm here by now. I take a step back and launch my heel to the right of the knob, shattering the doorjamb and sending wood splinters flying. The door swings open, letting in a thin slice of light that isn't enough to reveal anything. Straining my eyes in the darkness, all I can make out is a yellow sign of a man slipping on his ass amidst a pool of water with a mop tucked into a bucket marked Caution: Wet Floor. All useless clues as to who left these footprints in the carpet, so I push the door a little farther open.

As the sliver of light pushes deeper to the back of the closet, a pair of bright eyes appears. A girl my age, nineteen or twenty, darts out of the shadows and lunges at me with a knife. Instinctively, I twist my body to evade the blade by an inch. Within a few moments, I manage to subdue her and restrain her arm until it's bent fully behind her back. Then I kick her in the back of her leg, making her drop onto her knees on the soggy floor. Drawing my own blade, I hold its sharp point against her throat. The scent of jasmine fills my nose.

"Don't kill me! Please don't kill me!" she cries.

I stop. Either she's the first Eater to talk, or I've finally gone mad. With a firm grip on her arm, I look around to see her face. Her lips are full and ripe, and her teeth are whiter than snow. Her eyes are large and brown, with no bloodshot veins running through them. Skin smooth and fresh. Her hair is as dark as night and pulled back in a ponytail. Her clothes aren't clean but aren't disgustingly dirty either. They seem more like day-hike attire than normal winter wear. Against my usual judgment, I let her go. She stands up.

"Who are you? What the hell do you want?"

"Who am I?" I put my knife back in its sleeve. "Who the hell are you? There's no way you're living here. With those clothes, you'd freeze to death. Are you from the village?"

"I'm not saying! I'll tell you this, though. My friends are coming back so you might wanna get out of here."

"Did you claim this building or something?"

"No!"

"Well, why do I have to get out of—?"

"Are you from Ghost Village?" she blurts out before I can finish my question.

"Ghost Village? No, I'm from nowhere. I'm on my way to the village about three klicks up this trail."

"What's a klick?"

"It's a kilometer."

"You mean Hill Top Village. Why do you wanna go there?"

"I have some things to trade." I put both my thumbs under the straps of my backpack, lift the bag, and then drop it back down. From her calmer voice, I can tell she is starting to understand who I am.

"What's your name?" she asks.

I hesitate for a moment. It's clear she isn't part of the Red Empire's forces. Should I give her my real name, or an alias? I'd like someone to know who I really am, for once. But I don't answer.

I can hear two people talking outside the door with no regard for how loud they are. I tense up; there's no time to hide. One voice is louder than the other. I can't make out what they're saying, but it's so loud it sets me on edge.

Their steps are heavy. Stepping on every branch and twig on the ground, telling me they are civilian survivors. Silhouettes appear in the threshold. Two teenagers walk inside. One has a well-chiseled face with self-cut hair, wearing tattered day-hiking clothes. The other has an unkempt face with out-of-control shaggy hair. He's as thin as a starved Eater, but there is life in his eyes. When he sees me, he steps backward, putting his back against the wall. The fear lets me know he isn't a problem. As for the other boy, his posture changes from surprised to tense once he sees my rifle.

"Jaysi, get behind me!" he screams.

I respond with an aggressive, "Shhhhh. You can't be yelling like that out here." I know with that bleeding elk limping around, Eaters aren't far behind.

"JAYSI!!" he yells even louder.

Jaysi tries to calm him. "Kyle. He just wants to trade with us."

Kyle ignores Jaysi's soft voice.

"Yeah, Kyle, just relax," I say.

"Relax? You have a gun! Only the Red Empire has guns. That's the shot we heard earlier. Who did you kill?"

I drop my bag. It hits the ground with a giant thud. I point to it.

"I have quarters of elk meat I want to trade. That's it. Then I'll be on my way."

Kyle walks a little closer to inspect the bag. My eyes catch movement a little past the doorway. I try to keep my attention on Kyle, while my ears stay focused on the outside noises.

Kyle says, in his loud voice, "You need to pick up your bag and get gone."

I lift my hand in Kyle's direction, motioning for him to stop moving. I put my index finger up to my tightened lips. "Shhhh."

"Don't tell me to 'shhhh.' I'm not—"

Before he can get the last word out, three Eaters storm in. The one leading the pack has third-degree burns on every part of his body; his skin is a charred, melted mess and lacks any sign of hair. His military-issued camouflaged pants hang off him loosely, barely covering his lower half. His one eye stares at me with an extreme intensity.

The other one is female. She has a freshly gnawed right arm that's missing from the elbow down, unknowingly bleeding to death. She's dressed like a librarian or a businessperson. A flowing, off-white business blouse, half-tucked into charcoal gray pleated pants. I can tell she hasn't eaten in a long while. She is slow-moving.

The last one is the same age as me. He looks recently turned, with missing lips and fresh blood flowing from his tongue. Kyle recoils in shock and horror. It's clear none of them will be of any help.

I clench my fists and tighten my grip on my knife handle as the lava-faced military Eater charges toward us. With one swift movement, my blade slices through his jugular. He crashes into the wood-paneled wall hard enough that I hear a crack. Thankfully, there is concrete beneath the paneling causing his neck to break. His body lies still, indicating that he is no longer a threat.

The librarian seems the weakest and so I unleash a roundhouse kick to her chest, which sends her soaring over the warped desk, first smashing into the office chair then slamming into the wall. A chunk of wooden paneling smashes into her head as the chair flips backward. With her temporarily out of the way, I'll have a chance to take care of this newly turned Eater. Newborn Eaters always have energy, which makes them dangerous.

He doesn't rush me at first. As he gets a little closer, he lunges at me. The one good thing about Eaters is they aren't patient enough to wait for the right moment. All they have on their minds is food. As he lunges, I counter his weight with my free hand, throwing him off balance. Behind him now, I extend my hand upward, driving the blade of my knife through the soft spot in the back of his skull. It slides in with ease. Holding tight to my knife, the kid lifts his arms in a Frankenstein fashion. Almost like he's reaching for me even though I'm behind him. Holding the knife handle, I feel like I'm holding him up like a puppeteer.

I attempt to remove my knife from the kid's head. It's more difficult than I thought it would be, no matter which direction I try pulling in. In an act of desperation, I thrust my boot forward and kick him as hard as I can on his back. My foot smashes against his spine. He catapults forward so fast that my knife finally comes free from his head. He crashes into the already-dead burnt Eater below.

The woman Eater is lumbering toward me, even weaker now. Throwing my knife is my first instinct, but if I miss, my survival chances drop. She lifts her nub and her other arm, trying to grab me. She must think her missing forearm and hand are still attached to her elbow. I bet she's imagining my face like an ear of corn. Holding my ears and nibbling away at my face.

I shift to the side of her body that was missing a hand. Then, without wasting a moment, I drive my knife straight into her temple with one swift motion. Easiest Eater kill ever! Her head drops onto her shoulder. It takes quite a bit of effort to get a blade through a human skull—even if it belongs to an Eater. Once the handle is released from my grip, she thuds face-first onto the floor. Death's peculiar: you expect them to put their hands out and break their fall, but instead, limbs remain limp and unresponsive as gravity pulls them in its direction. Her teeth collide with the ground first, causing them to break and ricochet toward Kyle's feet.

Kyle looks away when he sees the pink-stained teeth. My eyes remain on Kyle as I stride over to the woman and place my heel down onto her skull. With a firm grip, I pull my knife out of her head. There's an unsettling sound when my blade slides free from the bone that sends chills down my spine and causes me to twitch. No matter how much it unsettles me, I maintain my focus on Kyle. He appears scared, while Jaysi simply asks, "Who are you?"

I point my knife at Kyle. He takes a few steps back.

I say to him: "You can't be yelling out here. You're just ringing the dinner bell for Eaters."

I slide my blade on the woman Eater's blouse and wipe the blood off it. Her off-white silk collar quickly turns red with a few swipes from the knife. I sheathe the knife and hoist my backpack on, attempting to pretend it's not heavy. I feel my legs strain as I step through the doorway to leave. The others follow to catch up. The skinny one is still curious.

"Seriously. Who are you?"

I respond with my own set of questions.

"What are y'all doing out here? You have no survivor skills! You're not even dressed for winter."

Pushing the blame, he responds, "It's Jaysi's fault! She always wants to explore old buildings. She's always looking for things from the past."

Already feeling like too much information was being given, Kyle grunts through his unmoving lips. "Shut up, Stick!"

A perfect name for such a skinny guy. Jaysi looks at me and admits her curiosity. "It's true. I'm an Archivist."

"An Archivist?" I respond. "What's that?"

"They call me the Keeper. I collect stories and keep them archived at the village. I have tons of personal accounts of passersby and traders. It keeps us informed on what's happening beyond the woods. The more informed we are, the better our survival. Plus, everyone has a story, right? Why not learn from it? That's what I do. I collect pieces of the past. Since we can't surf the Internet anymore, we have to get our information somehow. I also hunt for books, maps, and—"

"History?" I interrupt her. "What in the past will change our situation right now? Why learn about something you can't do anything about?"

"We need to learn from the past. We need to keep records, so our children and our children's children know what to do or what not to do. They need solutions if the same problems come up. We can give them that experience. Our records will help make their decisions easier."

Laughing, I look at Jaysi. "Children's children? The Red Empire won't let that happen. They're exterminating us!"

T he snow doesn't stick to the used, mud-filled trails that wind through the small village. The pathways are eerily reminiscent of the ditches where I fought day after day during the war. I think about how easy it would be to drop a few rocks and mulch into the ground and use them as steppingstones. Still, my attention is drawn to the poorly built shacks that line the mud path. Amongst these rickety shacks stand two magnificent log cabins made from white pines. Although they may be old, these cabins are the lifeblood of this village. The elegant craftsmanship indicates they were a summer retreat for an affluent family many years ago. A thin wisp of smoke curls up from the river rock chimney. On the north side of the house, a bit of green mildew has begun to form, providing an extra millimeter of insulation against the cold.

The huts, however, drunkenly lean to one side, with gaps so large I could fit my fist through them. Knots and uncut branches protrude from the logs. Almost like they were purposely left to stab or scratch anyone that came too close.

Inside one of them, a small fire burns in a circle of stones on the ground inside, casting an orange glow that creeps out from the cracks. The person inside is sitting on a tree stump stoking the fire. She seems content with her living arrangement. Still, it isn't any more luxurious than the nights I spent in hollow trees. At least there, I had a way out if danger came calling.

Behind the two cabins is a large old tobacco barn made of red cedar. It is one of the largest barns I've ever seen. It appears to be their storage facility, the way the villagers walk in with empty hands and exit holding dry firewood, tools, and clothes. The whole village comprises eighteen to twenty people. There are more boys than girls. The girls appear to be nervous about me being here. They whisper amongst themselves and keep their distance. The boys look me up and down as if I'm a threat. I am mystified by the girl/boy ratio especially since most boys were killed in the war.

I follow Jaysi to the first log cabin. The heat radiating from the room wraps itself around me when I step inside. At first, its warmth is pleasant, but soon it begins to suffocate me; I hadn't been in such intense heat during the winter months in years. Living in the woods, I am used to sitting by fires—my front side burning while my backside freezes. I would alternate between flipping myself over and back again, but this heat has no escape.

Stick strides to the fireplace and drops the armful of firewood he gathered on the path. No wonder people call him Stick; his job is to collect firewood. I must admit that I admire that role—how important it must be to keep everyone warm during the chilly winter months. If I had the job, I know I'd take great pride in it.

The fireplace has been built with the same gray river rock as the chimney outside. Each stone has been carefully cut and fit together like a jigsaw puzzle, creating a perfect pattern that runs up the wall. The mouth of the fireplace is large enough for me to stand in without hitting my head, and the fire burns so hot it lights up the dark room like daylight. Flames lick at the sides, emitting intense heat that could cook a meal if one were brave enough to withstand it.

The cabin is well-maintained and has all the furnishings from the old days. Pictures of the old homeowner still hang on the wall. The images are a little cloudy and damaged by the moisture, but the three kids still seem to smile through the dull colors. One picture is of parents kneeling beside the kids, smiling just as big, standing in front of a waterfall. It's a familiar backdrop. I know I've seen that waterfall before. The way they are smiling, it must have been a proud moment for that family. A polished piece of ash wood rests on the fireplace's mantel with *As for me and my house, we will serve the Lord*" carved in the center. I don't know if the sign was from the family in the picture or the ones occupying it now. Jaysi notices me taking it all in.

"That's what I want," Jaysi says. "I seem to have forgotten what my parents look like. I want my children to see me grow old like the people in that picture."

"Old people," I say.

Kyle comes in behind us and stays near the door. Three men turn to face me at a rustic dining room table. The first one stands and extends his hand for me to shake. He has long hair and a full beard. They aren't old but they aren't young.

"I'm Mac! Local inventor and advisor to the board."

With no threat, I decide to give them my real name instead of an alias.

"Drift."

"Pleased to make your acquaintance, Drift."

The next man to stand up is of a short, round stature, and his presence is immediately noticeable. He has shorter hair and a red balloon face. His outstretched arm has sweat beads running down it. When he extends his hand, I put mine inside of it. It feels clammy and puffy. When we release our grips, I immediately want to wipe it on my pant leg.

"Number Two."

"I'm sorry?" I reply, a little confused.

"The village calls me Number Two."

"Why Number Two?"

"We are a republic village with elected officials. I'm what you would call second in command or Vice President of the community."

"Well, pleased to meet you, Number Two. Why don't you just use your real name?"

"When my term is over, I will use my real name, but for now, Number Two is my name. It reminds the villagers that we are a civil society. The village people voted on my name being Number Two, so that's what it is."

I extend my hand to the third man. He's a good-looking man with no scars, no missing limbs, and no holes in his clothes. A five-o'clock shadow covers his face, and he wears it well. His grip is firm and steady.

"You must be Number One," I say in a serious voice. He laughs under his breath and reaches out his hand.

"Yes. Villagers call me Number One. You can just call me Benjamin or Ben."

"Drift…nice to meet you."

"Pleasure's all mine. Now, what brings you to Hill Top Village?"

"Trade." The one word I know he wants to hear.

I make my way to the wooden farm table and drop my overly stuffed backpack. As soon as it leaves my back, I feel relief wash over me. A big, circular sweat patch, coincidentally the same shape and size as my backpack, remains on my body. The cool air against that part of my back feels wonderful, while the rest of me still struggles with the heat. Number Two then approaches the bag to try lifting it himself. He tugs on it but can only budge it by an inch or two before gravity reclaims it from his grip. A low grunt escapes from him.

"What's in the bag? Why's it so heavy?" With another attempt, he stands the bag upright.

To save him the trouble, I unzip the top of the backpack, revealing a few black garbage bags.

"Meat!" I pull the first one out and untie the top of the bag to showcase a few large squares of meat.

Ben looks in amazement, asking, "Was it contaminated?"

"My meat is never contaminated."

"We haven't seen good meat around here in a while," Number Two says.

"I shot her about a day and a half east of here. There's meat out there. It just takes a lot of patience."

Ben looks at the rifle on my shoulder. He reaches out to touch it.

"Don't!" I say.

Stick smiles. "Trust me, you do not want to touch that."

Number Two moves around me like a shark ready to attack its prey. I reluctantly let him circle me, and he raises his hand, disregarding my rules, as if to touch the rifle. Stick quickly prevents him from doing so.

"Seriously, you don't want to do that."

Number Two tilts his head.

"Is it on the GRID? Won't they find us?" he asks.

"It's too old to be on the GRID," I respond with a smirk, but I understand why he's concerned.

Before the war, the GRID, which is short for the Gun Recognition Identification Department, had set up a digital cloud system to keep track of firearms. Politicians saw an easy way to make money by bringing in new gun companies and software developers because of the number of gun owners. Every law-abiding gun owner needed to follow the decree. Law enforcement compelled people to hand over their firearms. Law enforcement destroyed old guns as they collected them. They promoted a gun for a gun. A new GRID-certified gun for your old one. If you didn't want to trade, they offered cash. They ran countless ads trying to convince people it was better for our society. They said crime rates would plummet. The new guns had computer chips and embedded RFIDs, which GRID tracked in real time. If the chip was removed, the gun wouldn't fire. It was that simple. These GRID guns were equipped with live tracking technology and DNA readers. Whenever someone wrapped their palm around the handle, it would register on GRID's switchboard. Even if the gun shook or moved, it would register. When the trigger was pulled, a GPS pin drop was logged along with the DNA of whoever pulled it. It kept track of how many bullets were fired and what direction they went. GRID could shut off a gun during a mass shooting, if necessary, as an extra safety measure. It was a fantastic way to fight crime. Police could track the gun to whatever trash can or river it was dropped in.

The GRID worked like it was meant to. Keeping people responsible, the gun-related death rate plummeted to an all-time low. Everyone saw it as the best invention and security system ever created—at least for a while. Unfortunately, the built-in kill switch came back to haunt them. When then the Red Empire hacked into the GRID, all civilian guns became useless with one press of a button. All except guns like mine.

Before I got to basic training, there were a thousand relics in an old warehouse on the base. The guns were scheduled for destruction, but when the GRID shut down, and war broke out, those relics became the most valuable military assets on the base, other than the bodies they needed to carry them.

My Remington .308 rifle came from that warehouse. When they gave it to me, there were only four or five of its kind. I chose to call my rifle Sophia.

"He took out three Eaters in like six seconds. I've never seen anything like it. It was incredible," Jaysi blurted out.

"Were you in the military? How did you get to keep this rifle?" Ben asks.

"I walked off the front line with it. Everyone else was dead, so it seemed like a waste to leave it."

"You were on the front line? I'd love to hear your story and what kind of gun it is." Jaysi said.

"It's a sniper rifle. No GPS. No serial numbers. No name attached to it, just a good old-fashioned untraceable sniper rifle. It's an antique. The real problem with this gun is lack of bullets. Without bullets, this thing's just a paperweight."

Jaysi steps up. "Bullets? We have bullets! Maybe we can trade: meat for the bullets. They've been in the barn forever."

"Quiet, Jaysi! We have no idea who this man is. He could be with the Ghost Village for all we know." Number Two says.

My heart races, anticipating the possibility that the village may have my .308 caliber bullets in stock. If not, I could make new ones with the empty casings in my pouch.

I'm not familiar with the Ghost Village. Maybe they call it a Ghost Village, while I call it Loco Solo.

"You mean the Loco Solo village?" I respond.

Number Two laughs. "That's no Loco Solo village. I assure you."

"When I passed by it, it sure smelled like one. From where I was, I saw cages filled with Eaters too."

"Those people are alive. They aren't Eaters!" Number Two says.

"Well, I don't belong to any Ghost Village. I live out there"—I look out the window and point to the tree line— "in the woods, by myself. I avoided them because I thought they were Loco Solos. If you have bullets, then I'll trade the meat for them."

Ben walks over to the bag of meat and pulls the lid open again.

"Bullets are rare, Drift! It's going to take more than a bag of meat to get the bullets."

Knowing it's negotiation time, I ask Ben. "Do you have guns?"

"No," he says.

"Then why are they so important to you?"

"Ah. It's because they're so important to you, Drift, that it will take more than meat."

"First, I see the bullets, and then we discuss the terms. You might not even have the caliber I need."

Mac speaks up. "He makes a good point." Mac looks to the front door of the cabin. "Let's go and see, shall we?"

I follow Mac, Jaysi, Kyle, and Stick, with Number One following behind us to the tobacco barn. The floor is covered with wood chips, and a few teenage boys are busy splitting cedar logs in preparation for another shack. Even though it smells musty and old in there, I find the scent oddly pleasant because it still hints at the sweet aroma of dried tobacco and newly cut cedar. My first thought is that those wood chips would make a good option on the mud path outside, but then I am drawn to one side stall filled with metallic objects, pipes, and wires. Mac notices my curiosity.

"That's my work area. That's where the magic happens," he says.

I'm curious about what Mac makes with all his materials, but I stay on-task. We approach a tarp in the corner of the barn, and Mac pulls it away to reveal a large pile of dented green Army crates.

"We found them in a crashed truck at the bottom of a ditch. You know, one of those old antique ones with actual wheels. It took us three days to carry these crates back here," Mac says.

As I approach the boxes, my eyes widen. I carefully trace my fingers over the words printed on one of the boxes. u.s. army .308 caliber is emblazoned on the side.

"This box," I say.

Kyle and Stick head toward the boxes and lift the ones on top. After they maneuver their way down to the one I asked for, it proves too heavy for either to move alone. Joining forces, they drag it out to the middle of the barn. Everyone gathers around the box while I kneel to take a closer look.

"Good luck with that," Kyle said. "We've been trying to open these boxes for years. We've broken every tool we used trying to pry them open."

I don't bat an eye at Kyle's remark and instead focus on the sunken dial to the right of the box. I rotate it clockwise before pushing it in, causing the lid to become transparent. Everyone takes a step back from it. Every bullet is stacked perfectly inside, like an honor guard of soldiers in an orderly line. The brass casings are bright and gleaming; they look freshly made. I try to remain composed, not wanting anyone to guess how badly I want them. They could ask for the moon, and I'd be willing to shoot it out of the sky. "How d'you know to do that?" Jaysi asks.

"It's a soldier thing."

I run my hand across the top of the box in amazement of the abundance of ammo. Stick walks up to the box and tries to reach his hand inside, but it buckles when it hits the transparent Switchable top. He tries again and again but just smudges the see-through glass.

"I can't get to 'em, but I can see 'em."

"They're still inside the box," I tell Stick.

Standing up, I look at Number One.

"I'll take 'em. I'll take 'em all."

Kyle laughs. "How are you going to carry this box through the woods? It took me and Stick all we had just to lift it."

Crouching back down, I press another concealed button, which reveals a touchscreen panel on the top of the transparent lid. The numbers are aglow in a muted neon green. I type in 8275 #, and the box rises waist high. I put my palm flat against it and step forward, causing the box to float effortlessly across the ground in front of me.

"That would have come in handy a year ago," Mac remarks. "Can you show us how to do that so we can open more of these boxes?"

"I'll show you—for this box of bullets."

"I knew you would say something like that, but we're gonna need more than a lesson in box levitation," Mac responds.

Stick runs up to the box and slides his hand under it. The levitating box amazes him.

"I thought HUVs weren't able to fly," Stick said.

"This isn't a HUV. These are off GRID," I answer.

"I could put all my wood in one of these boxes and carry a hundred times what I carry now," Stick says.

The other villagers catch sight of the hovering box and pause to observe. We walk to the cabin, and Jaysi eagerly runs up to the door and holds it open for us.

Number Two gawks at the emerald coffin box as it enters the door. He jumps back, nearly toppling his chair in the process. His fear dissipates when a group of people walk in behind the container. I enter a code onto the LED numerical pad, causing the strange container to drop to the floor. Number One strides over to join Number Two's side. Not knowing what the trade will be, I start the negotiations.

"What do you want for the bullets?" I ask.

"Protection!" Number One says.

"I'm not a bodyguard. I'm a hunter."

"A good one at that. You're military-trained, and you seem well educated in survival. I need at least three months of service from you to help teach and protect this community."

"Three months? I haven't stayed in one place that long since the war."

"The Ghost Villagers attack us regularly, especially throughout the winter. They steal the stockpiles we work so hard on all summer. They even come in the middle of the night and steal the girls. The head of their tribe is some old Asian man with white hair."

"White hair?" I ask.

I've heard of a man with white hair. The Grey Wolf. A sniper for the Red Empire that supposedly died in the war.

"Yeah, the kids in his village pretend to be him by coloring their hair and face with white clay. You need you to teach us how to protect ourselves."

"One month. And you feed me while I'm here."

"Two months, and we'll feed you, and you'll show Mac how to open the cases in the barn."

Jaysi walks over to Number One and whispers in his ear.

He continues. "And you give the Keeper your stories for the village records."

"No stories! My past is mine and mine alone. Two months of protection and two months of food. I'll show Mac how to open the boxes, and I sleep in the barn."

Number Two interrupts. "You can have a cabin like everyone else."

I can't help but laugh. "Is that what you call those things: cabins? Like I said, two months and food. I'll show Mac how to work the boxes, and I sleep in the barn. Those little cabins are too out in the open. Someone could stab you with a spear through those fist-sized cracks."

I sink to the ground and type in a new code on the keypad. The lid of the box pops open with a hiss, as if it were an airlock being decompressed. I reach into the seemingly bottomless container and take out a hundred rounds of ammo. It doesn't even appear that I took anything from the stockpile, since there are still so many bullets left inside.

"No bullets until your job is complete," Number Two says.

"You want protection? These protect! Unless you expect me to throw sticks at people."

Stick looks at me, perplexed.

"Sorry, Stick. No disrespect."

Stick shrugs and puts more wood on the blazing fire.

Number Two answers, "How do we know you won't take those bullets and run?"

"I'd say you'd be getting the better end of the deal. If I run, you get all the meat on that table for a hundred bullets."

Standing and extending my hand to Number One, we seal the deal. As I close the lid to the box, Number Two says, "The box stays here."

"Fine with me."

The urge to take the hundred bullets and leave continuously crosses my mind. Everyone in this house will probably die sooner than later, anyways. I abandon the thought as Number One asks Jaysi to direct me to the barn. She fetches some bedding from one of the backrooms while I place all the meat from my backpack on the dining table. Once I have my bag, I follow her lead. When we reach the entryway, Kyle stands, blocking our way.

"Excuse me."

Kyle doesn't respond but steps out of the way. I don't even think about him because I'm so relieved not to be carrying that extra weight on my back. It feels like I am walking on air.

As we walk, Jaysi stares at me until she asks, "Why won't you give me your stories?"

"Because they're my stories."

"Do you have a girlfriend?"

She catches me off guard. I stumble over my words. "A... a, a what?"

"A girlfriend?"

"No! I'm solo out here."

"I figured you would have a girl. You trade with all the villages. Don't you have a girl at any of them? I'm just asking if you have somebody, that's all."

"No," I say firmly.

Perhaps it was the tone of her voice, or the fact that I am not a fan of socializing, but I found her question to be too upfront.

Mac follows us as we walk into the barn.

"They want me to bring all the Army boxes into the cabin. Number Two thinks you want to sleep in the barn because there's something you want in one of them."

"Sure," I respond.

I make the boxes weightless, and the teenagers who had been cutting wood walk them to the cabin. I then go to the spot they were originally in and use that as my bed. The area is dry, and the weight of the boxes left a nice, flat surface for me to sleep on.

Mac looks at me. "I get up early. I tinker all morning and into the night."

"Don't worry about me. I'll be awake. I'm always awake."

Mac looks at me intently. "We're living in the stone ages again. We have to boil water on fires just to make it safe. Doing dishes in the creek. With these inventions, I'm trying my best to change all that."

I respond. "The Red Empire wants it this way. They control us by limiting our resources. It's a genius strategy if you ask me. In a hundred years, maybe we'll be back on top. It's the cycle that is and always was."

Talking with Mac reminds me of all those "Feed the Children" ads when I was young. Commercials would come on TV, and my tiny brain couldn't comprehend why these impoverished kids had nothing but an infomercial. The United States had fancy robots, high-tech gadgets, and hovercrafts, while the children in these videos had empty stomachs, tear-filled eyes, and often bare feet. I couldn't figure out why those people were so far behind in technology, but now I know.

I've been lying down to rest while the boys work nearby, me-thodically cutting branches off fallen logs. I can't recall their names, so I think of them as Wood Chopper One and Two. They never speak much, but they are undoubtedly brilliant craftsmen at constructing horrible shelters. With that thought in mind, it might be smarter to sleep in one of their cabins; at least then, I might get some rest. Before my eyes can close again to ponder on that decision, the sound of chopping and hammering stops around me.

I get to my feet and move away from the barn. The boys slam down their axes in the log they were cutting and are now heading for the second cabin. Mac follows them closely. It probably means it's dinner time. I pause to tight-lace my boots up to my calves before venturing out. It's unbelievable that I can't remember the last time I was somewhere where I could take off my boots.

I hoist Sophia's strap over my shoulder. It hangs there, the butt of the gun resting atop my hamstring and the forestock lying along my shoulder blade. I imagine how it would feel to walk around without it. I assume it would be like the day my mom lost her wedding ring. She kept touching her finger and twisting the tan line where it once rested. I think that's how I'd feel if I was ever without my rifle: phantom sensations and a constant need to reach for it.

Following the other villagers, I step inside the second log cabin for the first time. It's arranged differently. This one is more of a dining hall. You could sit twenty-two people at each of the three tables. Unfortunately, there are only enough of us to sit around one and a half of them.

Jaysi spots me. She gestures toward the empty chair next to her. She looks different than when I first saw her. She's clean, and her hair is pulled back out of her eyes. She has dried flowers stuck in her hair. Walking over to her, I notice the table has a bunch of mismatched plates and glasses. All the glass is dull in color and cloudy. I always drink from a tin cup. Not many nomadic people carry glass in their bags.

Taking my seat next to Jaysi, I smell that familiar jasmine scent. I tell her she smells like a flower. Jaysi drops her head, tilts it a little.

"Are you ok?" I ask.

"Yeah," she responds. "Why wouldn't I be?"

"Your skin just turned pinkish."

"Oh, it's hot in here."

I have no reason to doubt her explanation. It's stuffy in the room. Out of the corner of my eye, I notice Number Two getting out of his chair and standing up. He holds an off-green glass in one hand and in the other a dull butter knife. He begins striking the blade against the glass, producing a loud *cling, cling, cling* that echoes through the room. Everyone stops their conversations to stare at him; he repeats it again: *cling, cling, cling.*

"Thank you to our guest Drift for bringing meat to the village. Our preparers of food made an incredible stew. Please get used to seeing his face. He will be staying with us for two months. Make him feel welcome."

Everyone applauds. It's uncomfortable. I put on the best fake smile I can. Once the applause stops, Jaysi taps my shoulder.

"It's hot in here. Your face is pinkish too."

Two girls fumble with a rusted cooking crane. The crane is anchored deep in the brick on the inside of the fireplace. The swinging iron arm reaches over the fire, holding a large black kettle. With an iron poker, the girls swing the hot kettle out of the fireplace. The squeaking arm of the crane is noticeable. As soon as the pot is close enough, the girls take the same poker and run it through the handle of the kettle. The girls are on opposite ends of the poker. They lift with all their strength and remove the kettle from the crane. Small sweat beads fall from one of their brows as they struggle with the pot and the heat. The kettle is so enormous that a whole deer could fit in it. They carry it to the table, their steps steady and slow. All around me, I can smell the delicious aroma—something I haven't smelled in years. When they lift the lid off with a pair of tongs, steam follows, twirling into the air above us before reaching its way to the ceiling. They pull out a ladle and scoop out a portion of stew. Each person passes a bowl to their right. The stew is full of meat and potatoes—I haven't seen a potato since we were on the front lines! There are also orange carrots, mushrooms, and green beans swimming throughout the bowls. As soon as they set the bowl in front of me, my mouth starts to water. It's hard not to show my excitement—if this is what we eat every night, then I definitely got the better end of this deal.

Once everyone has bowls of stew, Number One stands. "Let's bless the food."

Confused, I lay my spoon back down. Jaysi reaches over and grabs my hand. At the same time, the boy sitting on the other side of her takes hold of her other hand. Number One lowers his head and closes his eyes, and everyone else follows suit. As a result, I do the same.

"Heavenly Father, bless this food and have it nourish our bodies. Thank you for bringing Drift into our lives. Thank you for sending your one and only Son to die on the cross for our sins. In Jesus's name, we pray."

Everyone says, "Amen."

I remember in basic training, some people wanted to pray before eating but were sternly reprimanded by the drill sergeant. He always said, "Call out to the person next to you when you need help; it's my job to ensure you make it through this war. Prayer won't save you from a bullet." They released my hands much faster than they had reached for them and immediately picked up their spoons.

I remember the few kids that did it in silence. I never saw it as a bad thing. I just didn't understand it. One of them gave me his cross necklace and told me it would bring me good luck. I lost it during a 3:00 a.m. raid on a city one night. Serge was right, though. Prayer didn't stop bullets, or at least not the bullet that killed the boy who gave me the cross. The boy, though, was never afraid. He always seemed like he was going to a better place. Maybe we all thought we would go to a better place.

I notice that Stick isn't at the table.

"Where's Stick?" I ask.

I catch Jaysi in that awkward predicament of having just taken a bite of food but wanting to answer promptly. Steam comes from her mouth. The spoonful of hot stew puffs her cheeks out. She looks down in embarrassment and lifts her index finger, asking me to hang on a minute. After a few more chews, she swallows and then answers.

"It's his turn to be on watch."

"One boy to keep watch—there are four sides to the village. There's no way he can cover that much ground."

The door flies open, and Stick is at the door. He is wet from the recent snowfall. He looks at me. I want to offer him a bowl of stew to warm him up, but Number Two stands and yells.

"You, sir, are on watch. Get back outside and do your duty!"

He collapses to the ground. I see a large spear jutting out of his back as I look closer. Everyone panics and races to the rear of the cabin as I leap over the table and rushed toward Stick. Half his body illuminated by the light from within the cabin while the dark shadows from the night loom over the other half.

"He's dead."

I hear a rustling from one of the shacks in the village, and I realize that everyone else is in the dining hall. I crane my neck out into the night and scan my surroundings while muttering to myself.

"Well, this is what I signed up for. Time to go to work."

Without any second thoughts, I jump away from the porch steps. The warmth and light become a distant memory as the night wraps itself around me. As I creep closer to the source of the noise, I take each step with extreme caution. When I eventually reach the shack, I see two figures inside. The gaps between the logs make for easy viewing, but there is only one entrance—and it's where I am standing right now.

As they tear through the shack, my mind assesses who they could be. I'm certain they are not soldiers; if they were, they would have barricaded the dining hall and lit us all aflame. It cannot be thieves either, as they wouldn't make their presence so obvious or leave behind evidence like a spear in the back. The only option left is that these are scavengers. Scavengers travel from one place to another and take whatever is needed to survive—even lives. They know how to use their strength in battle because they fight so often. Their tricks have become second nature.

I pull my knife from its sheath and ready myself.

"Hey!" I whisper in their direction.

A sudden stillness fills the air before the splattering sound of things falling to the mud floor. The first scavenger makes a break for the exit. I'm taken aback as my knife sinks effortlessly into his chest—no one from this village had ever fought back against them. The scavengers are caught off guard.

The corpse falls to the ground. I want to take my knife back, but there's no time. The blade had gone through bone and pulling it out of bone isn't easy. The next scavenger is standing right behind the dead one, but he pauses when he sees his companion lying in the mud. Taking advantage of this momentary shock, I lunge forward to attack. With the palm of my hand, I throat-punch the scavenger. It was a solid hit; he drops his spear and grasps his neck, gasping for air. I realize he may not be an experienced fighter. A true scavenger would never let go of their only form of protection. I pick up the spear. In that brief moment, I almost feel pity, but then I remember Stick, and all of my mercy evaporates. I tighten my grip and with all my power, I thrust the spear forward. The sharpened point runs through the scavenger's hands, then his throat, before exiting the back of his neck. Blood pours out from his neck wound, forming tiny bubbles that trickle down his throat. His attempts to breathe fail as he struggles to get air into his lungs. A gurgling noise comes from the open wound, telling me everything I need to know.

I get a grip on the ankles of both scavengers. Dragging them through the mud is no small feat, yet I want to get them to the light for investigation. On my way to the dining cabin, I hear Jaysi hushing the villagers to assure them it's me. I drop them at the cabin entrance; Number Two says, "What did you do? You murdered two Ghost Villagers."

"What have I done? My job. These guys killed Stick!"

In the sliver of light, I see the two invaders' faces. They are in their late teens or early twenties. White streaks run through their hair. Dried mud or clay is caked on their faces. I've heard of people doing this for camouflage. I've also heard it can serve as insulation in severe cold. But according to Hill Top, they are mimicking their leader.

Both of their hands are wrapped with gauze bandages. I don't know why they would use medical supplies for such a purpose unless it was to keep their hands warm instead of using gloves. The wrapping on one of their hands is loose, so I remove it. As the fabric unwraps, a fresh burn mark becomes visible. It looks like a circle that's overlapped with an X—I don't recognize it. I look up at Number One to see if he knows what the symbol means.

Number One looks in awe at the lifeless bodies. "I have no idea. A gang or a tribal ritual of ownership, maybe?"

I study both bodies a little more. Besides the burns, they have cracked and calloused hands. This tells me they do the heavy lifting in Ghost Village. One has a few small, sharpened sticks along with a roll of twine in his pocket. The other has a knife that is long and sharpened. I guess I killed him so fast he didn't have time to pull it out. They are wearing shoes made of dog skin and tied with fraying rope. They didn't fight like military personnel.

"I'd say they are scavengers, but I don't know," I say.

Number Two takes it upon himself to repeat some of what I said but with a raised voice. "SCAVENGERS!"

The villagers gasp. I've encountered a few scavengers before. Their trading posts are filled with stolen junk. They lure you in and let you go through it all, picking out what you need. The minute you turn your back or take your eyes off them they bang you in the head, taking whatever, you brought to trade. Then they trade you to the Loco Solos.

I roll over the first body to inspect the other side, only to be met with a chorus of grunts and moans from the villagers. Once I move the second body to take a closer look, a spear whizzes past me, barely missing my ear as it embeds itself deep into the side of the cabin wall. Screams erupt inside the log cabin. Villagers run to the back of it in fear. I hear the intruders' heavy footsteps run deeper into the woods. It sounds like two people, max. I touch my rifle and glance at Mac; I can tell he is thinking of doing the same. I stop.

"All they needed to do is barricade that door, strike a match, and watch us burn. They must need the cabins or need you all," I say.

With no hesitation, Mac responds, "Or what's in the cabin."

That night, nearly all the villagers stay in the dining hall. I pace in the darkness for hours, keeping watch. By morning, my feet ache from being tense and on edge. As the sky grows lighter and stars are replaced by sunlight, my body shuts itself off from exhaustion. Mac and the woodchoppers stir first, and when I made my way to the barn, Mac realizes that I had been up all night. When he sees me entering my stall to rest, he gives instructions to the woodchoppers.

"Let's take the morning off, boys."

I wake at midday feeling rested, but hungry. I walk to the dining cabin where a pot of stew is waiting for me. I fill my belly.

Number One enters. "Thanks for keeping us safe last night."

"Not all of us," I say.

"Stick. Yes, he will truly be missed, but that wasn't your fault."

"I've never seen these people before. How is that possible? I walk these woods like no one else."

Number One sits across from me at the table. "Traders like you think they're Loco Solos, so they avoid them. I believe there's more to 'em, but I don't know what."

Weeks pass with no attacks. The villagers return to their normal lives. The memory of Stick is all but forgotten. Seems that's how it is these days. Maybe it's expected.

They asked me to teach a few villagers how to hunt, so I decide to use my hunting knowledge and drop some dried corn that I discovered in their barn. The goal was to attract whitetail or mule deer and maybe even another elk. I told them the importance of having the high ground and taking advantage of nearby camouflage. Every morning, I took small groups of villagers down to where the corn was and taught them about deer tracks when there were any, as well as the occasional rooted soil from wild hogs.

After I arrived though, it was like all the animal trails suddenly vanished. We searched deeper into the forest and came upon a mountain face, where we huddled to watch an empty clearing. Jaysi and a few others were with me. Out of the corner of my eye, I kept catching her looking at me, and each time when our eyes met, she flashed a wide smile my way. Even though I liked how jasmine smelled on her, I had asked her not to wear any perfume when hunting because it would make it easier for animals to detect us.

"I'm bored!" Kyle says as he throws down the stick he's been whittling.

"Shhhh. It's about patience and timing," I respond in a whisper.

Getting louder, Kyle says, "You'd be better off spotting an HUV or a drone out here before seeing any deer."

"Well, don't come hunting anymore!" Jaysi fires back.

Kyle gets madder. It's hard for me not to feel good when Jaysi gets mad at Kyle. I feel like I'm winning some hidden battle I'm not even fighting. Kyle stands up. When he does, I grab his belt and pull him back down.

"Don't give away our position. If the deer see you, all this waiting will be for nothing."

"Then let it be for nothing cause that's all we ever get out here with you!"

Kyle stands again, momentarily pausing before walking off. Jaysi whispers at Kyle with a squashed angry face.

"Kyle…Kyle!"

My gaze follows Kyle as he moves off in the direction of the village, craning his neck every few steps to see if Jaysi is trailing him. My eyes dart the other way when I see movement nearby. I yell out to Kyle.

"Kyle, stop moving."

He looks back. "Whatever! Now, your yelling is scaring the deer. I'm out of here."

Jaysi stands and goes running toward Kyle, but I grab her shoulder.

"No, don't move, Jaysi."

Lifting my gun, I take aim. Jaysi assumes I'm taking aim at Kyle.

"You can't shoot him."

Knowing I'm going to need to be calm for what's about to pop out of the leaves, I don't respond. Jaysi screams.

"Kyle, he's gonna shoot you!"

As soon as those words leave her mouth, Kyle turns and looks back, seeing the barrel of my rifle aimed in his direction.

"Go ahead, murderer! Shoot me!" Kyle screams.

Before he can finish talking, a T8 appears from the leaves. It stands on its hind legs. Jaysi takes notice of the T8.

"Kyle, a robot…bug…thing!" she stutters.

Kyle falls backward onto his butt when he sees the metallic tic, placing him squarely in my line of fire. All I can see is the back of his head. Under my breath, I continue counting. Kyle's so close to the T8, the acid will eat right through him if I don't get this shot off.

"Six one thousand, seven one thousand… Kyle, move!"

Kyle is frozen. Any other person would run as fast as they could in the opposite direction. He can't find his fight-or-flight response.

Jumping to my feet, I run around so I can see the T8. It's not the ideal angle, but it's all I have. My first shot hits to the right of the red dot. A huge spark and a loud ding ring out. The bullet reflects off its armor and hits a tree to the side of it. I got lucky it didn't ricochet and hit Kyle. I put another bullet in the chamber, exhale, and hold my breath. I line the crosshairs up with the red dot.

"Twelve one thousand, thirteen…"

I pull my trigger finger back. *Peeuwoooooo.* Direct hit. The T8 explodes right in front of Kyle, causing shards of hot metal to fly toward him. His clothes smolder, and his face blisters from the raining hot metal. In a panic, he crawls away from the T8, screaming.

"I can't see. I can't see!"

Jaysi runs to his side. "It's ok! You're ok! Drift shot the bug."

"I can't see! My face…it burns!" he cries. "Get me back to the village!"

Jaysi grabs his arm and helps him to his feet. Kyle wraps his arms around her neck to get a better balance as she guides him back to the village.

I'm about to move forward with them when I hear cracking twigs behind me. I whirl around to see someone from Ghost Village sprinting away in the opposite direction. The trees are too close together for me to get an accurate shot off. Even though I have plenty of bullets left, my first reaction is to keep from wasting them. My second thought is to fire blindly into the forest, but I quickly realize that would be useless. So, reluctantly, I lower my weapon and allow the figure to escape.

When we return to the village, a crowd gathers around Kyle to help him into the second log cabin. Seeing that he is in good hands, I make my way to the barn, where Mac is running around his workstation and the teenage boys are busy cutting their wood. When I reach my sleeping quarters to rest, Mac strikes up a conversation.

"Well?"

"Well, what?" I respond with a little anger in my voice.

"Are we gonna be eating fresh meat tonight or what?"

"Oh! No. Not tonight. I was too busy putting a bullet through a T8."

Mac shakes his head. "Damn, I wish they would recall those things. The war is over. What good are they at this point?"

Mac had it right. The Man-O-War was a thing of the past. Technology like the T8 shouldn't have existed in the first place. The Biological Weapons Convention mandates were supposed to keep weapons like that from existing. But like everything else in politics, if you throw a little money that way, a blind eye is turned. At the start of WWIII, cannons and bullets were enough to get by.

"Did you kill it?" Mac asks.

"Yeah, I got it. It exploded right in Kyle's face, though. He's burned up pretty bad."

"Is he ok?"

I shake my head. "He just froze. He didn't run or get out of the way. He just froze."

"Is he ok?" Mac asked again.

"He was breathing when I left him at the cabin. He's being looked after."

I stand and walk over to Mac's station.

"Mac, do you trust me?"

Mac looks at me curiously. "I do."

"Jaysi thought I was gonna kill Kyle. I've never felt so untrusted. Jaysi yelled out, *He's gonna shoot you* to Kyle."

"Drift, she just knows how much you and Kyle hate each other. I'm sure everything happened really fast, and nobody was thinking straight."

"I was thinking straight," I said.

"Yeah, but you're trained to think under those conditions."

"As soon as I'm done here and I get those bullets, I'm out. No more drama. No more Kyle. I'm back to being on my own."

Mac leans over and drops a handful of sand down a large cylinder. The sand is fine and white.

"Don't be in such a hurry to leave, Drift. Some decisions take time. You'd do well in a community like this."

Not wanting to hear any more advice, I change the subject.

"So, what are you making? All I hear is you banging and bending metal day in and day out."

Mac's face lights up with excitement. Maybe because someone wants to actually talk about his work.

"A filtration system," he responds. "I want to filter the creek water so we don't have to boil it all the time. A big barrel of freshwater always ready for consumption."

"Gravel, sand, charcoal," I said.

Mac looks at me in surprised. "Exactly! You know about filtration?"

"I know enough to help, but I won't be around long enough to finish your project."

7

Awakening to the sound of Mac pounding away on the metal tube, I grimace. After standing watch most of the night, he has no sympathy for my need to rest. His strokes are more forceful this morning. As he looks my way while thumping, he is clearly doing it on purpose. He's not even bothered by all the times he misses the target.

"All right, all right! I'm up," I say.

I've just gotten into a sitting position, and before I can blink, Jaysi appears and invites Mac and me to the large cabin for a meeting. We both get up and follow her inside. Number One is sitting at the table with an enormous grin appearing as soon as he sees us. He heartily welcomes us into the room.

"Drift! Come in. Come in. I'd like to talk to you about something. I know we asked you to protect the village, but I was wondering."

Jaysi is restlessly walking back and forth. I'm sure she knows what Number One is about to ask me. It must have something to do with her, perhaps Kyle as well. Are they going to try to break off our agreement? Meat has been so scarce lately, and they haven't been raided in a while. Watching Jaysi nervously move around makes me anxious—which is strange since I'm usually not one to be intimidated.

"We want to grow this community," Number One continues. "We want to expand our horizons—"

"What do you want?" I blurt out. I hate when people beat around the bush.

"Jaysi and Mac think it would be a good idea to go to the nearest library and get some books for the village."

"Books!? You want to go into the city for books? Eaters and Red Empire soldiers are in the city. That's why we aren't."

"It's not just for books," Jaysi says. "It's our future. We can learn from those books. Mac can get books that explain how to invent things. Connor can get books on carpentry…" The tension in her voice builds as she mumbles on until she completes her statement with, "I'm going with or without you!"

"Calm down," Number One says with a soothing voice. "Jaysi, Mac, Kyle, and Connor are going, and I can't stop 'em. I've already tried. Drift, we've never had someone like you, someone with your skills. It's the first time we've even considered going into the city. I'd like for you to go."

"Is Kyle's face even healed enough to go? The city's no joke. Is one of us dying worth a book? Let's say we make it to the library. How do we know if there are any books left? Most buildings that held any educational value went up in smoke during the war. The Red Empire made sure of that. Wasn't that their goal? Keep us stupid, and them smart. They get HUV's and heaters, and we have feet and fires. They get guns, and we get sticks."

"Even if there's one book, it's worth it!" Jaysi exclaims.

I look at Mac, who I've come to know as a rational decision maker.

"Mac, you're on board for this?"

Mac paces without making eye contact.

"Drift, I feel if we, as a village, are going to continue to grow and educate ourselves, it's a must. We don't have internet anymore. We're flying blind out here."

"I don't think you guys will even make it to the city. What if the village comes under attack while we're gone?"

Number One looks at Jaysi and then Mac. "I think we can manage for a few days. I just believe that it's worth the risk."

"I can't go into the city with a team that doesn't trust me. Kyle should probably stay. Jaysi, you should probably stay behind too."

Jaysi puts her hand on my forearm in an endearing way.

"Drift, I trust you. I always have. Don't let that one moment get in the way."

Jaysi's eyes looking at me like that causes something in my body to heat up. I turn to Number One.

"I'm not held responsible for anything that happens while I'm gone. And I am definitely not responsible if someone gets killed on this dumb mission."

"Agreed." Number One holds out his hand and smiles. I give his hand a reluctant shake and behold Jaysi's huge grin. Her beaming mouth forces her puffy lips into a thin line and reveals a perfect set of white teeth.

"Now?" I say.

"Why not?"

"We have no rations. We don't have a plan. We at least need a game plan."

"No better time than the present then," Jaysi replies.

"I'll need to lay my stuff out and make sure I have the right necessities," I say.

"I'll tell Connor and Kyle while you get ready. See you in an hour."

Jaysi rushes out of the log cabin with a skip-like step. I raise my voice so she can hear me through the door.

"I'll need to see everything you guys are packing."

Number One is smiling when I look back at him with a dumb-founded look.

"She's willing to die for books?" I said.

Number One shrugs. "She's the Keeper. What else does she live for?"

I step out of the cabin and make my way to the barn, with Kyle hot on my heels. Apparently, Jaysi had already updated him on the mission being given the go-ahead. As he walked beside me, I noticed the bandages are gone—his burns have healed, though they are still glowing red. He can't stop smiling—though, he didn't seem to understand the risks of going into the city.

"Why are you smiling?" I ask.

"I haven't seen a city in years. I'm hoping I can score a candy bar or a Coke or anything that has a sweet flavor. I'm excited be-cause it's something new to do!"

I think of Jaysi and how she had been so protective of Kyle on the hunt. Will she shout out a warning if any Eaters are nearby, attracting all of them? Eaters love loud noises. It drives them into a mad frenzy whenever they hear anything too loud. Walking into the barn, I find Jaysi and Mac sitting in my stall.

"Really?" I say.

"We've been ready for this since the day you came to Hill Top Village," Mac said. "I hope we can carry as many books as we can."

"Four people, three days. We each carry our own rations," I inform them.

Kyle reaches into his backpack and pulls out some elk jerky. "I brought this. Isabella, the cook, gave me a bunch of it for the trip."

Connor hits Kyle in the arm. "C'mon man, we ain't stupid. We know there's a thing happening there."

Embarrassed, Kyle responds, "A thing?"

"Yeah. A thing. You like her, right?" When Connor says this, Jaysi squirms in discomfort.

Kyle divides the jerky into five equal parts in hopes to get off the subject. Jaysi divides out the dried fruit she brought.

I arrange the items I am packing into my bag in a neat line on my bed. My hydration bladder, ammunition, some dried beef, and fruit. A cloth for cleaning Sophia. Three pairs of socks. And a short length of rope which I always carry in case I need to set snares.

"Before we head out, make sure you have everything that you need. That way, you don't have to stress about it when we're on the go," I say.

After I get done packing my backpack, I watch everyone pick up their items and stuff them in their bags.

Kyle says, "While you take them to get books, I'm gonna get a bunch of winter gear for the village. We're running low around here."

I can't argue with that. All the jackets have holes, and their boots are almost soleless.

"This trip won't be easy. It's cold so our bodies will need more calories, more than what is in our bags. We'll need to be on the lookout for food too. There's no screaming or yelling out there. Giving our position away just compromises the whole unit," I say.

"Unit?" Kyle asks.

"You know what I mean: us," I answer.

Mac picks up his backpack and straps it on. "We know what you meant. Let's move out!" he says, sounding like my old sergeant.

"Let's roll," Kyle adds.

We exit the barn and walk down the slushy mud trail. Bits of ice crunch beneath our feet. I realize we will all be sleeping on this soon. I think I've grown accustomed to the safety—and even comfort—of the barn. It has already become an odd, enjoyable habit.

The hike doesn't take as long as I thought, just half the night and the whole next day. It's now close to dark again, and we stop right outside of the city limits. I gaze at a deserted house and the giant sycamore tree outside it. Its limbs are shooting and sprouting out in all directions. One long branch stretches over the roof of the ground floor.

"I'm gonna climb up to that limb and break in through the second story window. I'll come back down and unlock the front door. You guys stay here," I tell everybody.

"What's wrong with the window right in front of us? Let's just break that one," Kyle says.

"If you break a window higher up, Eaters won't climb through it. It's harder for them to catch your scent. The higher you go, the better your chances of not being eaten. They can't climb. That's why I always choose the second-story of a house," I explain.

I climb up the tree. My old boots do their best to give me secure footing as I go. I take a few steps out onto the limb that hangs over the first floor, and my weight causes the wood to sag until it touches the shingles below. I leap off and land on the roof. The limb snaps back and returns to its usual resting spot. I make my way to the second-floor window and smash it with Sophia's rifle buttstock. The window implodes, and glass rains onto the floor inside and around my boots. Carefully, I clamber through the broken shards of the window.

I take a moment to reflect as I stand in the room. A man and woman lie dead, hands joined in a mutual embrace, on the king-sized bed. The one on the left has a revolver still clutched in its bony fingers. There's dried blood splatter all over the wall and the bed. A suicide—but that's what I can't understand. Why would anyone give up their life like this? Why not go out fighting against the Red Empire soldiers or Eaters?

After making my preconceived judgments and drawing my conclusions, I see a wheelchair in the corner. Too old for war. I remove the revolver from the grip of the one skeleton gently. I wipe away the dust and cobwebs on it and spin the cylinder. I find four bullets in it. That was four more rounds of ammunition than I expected. Finding an off-GRID relic is rare, especially with bullets. Next to the bed is a nightstand. I pull the drawer handle in hopes of finding a box of ammunition.

When I do, six dusty brass bullets roll from the back of the drawer. It's not a box, but I'll take the six. I grab the bullets and pocket them.

Cobwebs fill each corner of the abandoned house, and a thick layer of dust blankets everything. It even sticks to my clothes as I disturb things. Footprints are left behind me as I descend the stairs, likely the first human to touch this place since the Man-O-War began. Unlocking the back door, I crack it open and let out a soft whistle. Everyone comes through the door one at a time. Once inside, we stir up more dust within the house, creating an effect that seems to make it look as if the house was haunted by spirits, the dust swirling in the fading daylight coming from the window.

The first stop is the kitchen. Kyle checks for anything with sugar, but nothing appears. The only edible option is some canned soup, so we take it and eat it cold from the can. The rat-chewed cracker boxes are too far gone to be salvaged. After eating, we head upstairs to look for a place to sleep, passing by the room where the two skeletons rest, I see the footprints I left behind. I skip by that room.

Mac and Connor take a room with two double beds. The decor is pretty much what you'd expect in a grandma's house—lots of doilies, rickety bedspreads, and vases with flowers. Jaysi, Kyle, and I take the room with a queen-sized bed, walls plastered with NFL posters, and images of guys swinging bats. The other wall is covered with pages from a magazine featuring models in bikinis. I get close to one picture to get a better look and then start coughing. I start choking on the dust.

"Serves you right!" Jaysi says playfully.

I can't believe my eyes. A girl wearing next to nothing is something I haven't seen in a while. It won't leave my head. I start imagining what Jaysi would look like in a bikini like that.

I come back to fast reality when she asks, "Are you done yet?"

I clear my throat and blame the dust. "I, I got dust in my eyes and throat. That's all."

We settle into the beds for the night. It feels good to sleep on a mattress: the same one Jaysi is on. Kyle sleeps on the floor.

I fall asleep, my mind filled with images of Jaysi in a barely-there outfit. When I wake up, my hand is resting on her hip. It's the most exquisite, softest feeling I've ever felt. I slowly open my eyes and quickly remove my hand before she notices. Kyle is already sitting up, his eyes open, and sees me.

"Nice job."

Jaysi stirs, and I spring out of bed, still wearing every stitch of clothing, including my boots. It's how I sleep in this environment—prepared to move or fight at a moment's notice. Then we make our way down the stairs. Everyone searches for food one last time, the daylight revealing more than before. While everybody is busy exploring, I pass Mac the revolver.

"Where did you get this?"

"It was upstairs. You know how to use it?"

"Damn right—no. Not really."

I reach into my pocket and hand him the other bullets I found. He inspects the gun. I can tell it is his first time holding such a relic.

"It's heavy as hell," Mac said.

I show him how to pull the ejector rod. I take the two spent bullets out and replace them with new ones. He catches on quick. I'm sure his mechanical brain makes it easier for him to understand. He takes a few minutes to check it out.

"That's why I never made it to the front line, you know. I could never kill anyone, but maybe I could kill an Eater. They aren't human. They can't be."

"You've seen Eaters. You know what they are," I say.

"I remember when my nieces turned. After the Man-O-War, I found my sister and her family barricaded in an underground shelter. We all agreed to go farther into the mountains when we ran out of supplies. One night we all fell asleep in my brother-in-law's tent. A T8 found us in the evening and let its gas go. My nieces snuck out of the tent to use the restroom and walked right into a cloud of gas. I woke up to the sound of teeth biting through bone. There were no screams, just the sound of open mouths smacking and chewing. The kids ate right through their parents' throats. A human wouldn't do that, right? I could have killed 'em with the machete, but I didn't. I slid out of the tent and zipped them in it. I just left them. I'm not sure why I didn't turn into an Eater. Maybe I'm immune? Maybe I'm lucky. Maybe the tent acted like a filter. I wish I knew."

"Listen, Mac," I tell him. "We have all had our share of encounters. I don't know if they're human or not. But I do understand one thing is certain—this firearm. If you are on the receiving side of those teeth, it'll protect you and may very well keep you alive."

Mac bounces the gun in the palm of his hand. Practices lifting it as if he is going to shoot it.

"Impressive craftsmanship," is all he can say.

Mac's comment about Eaters being human echoes in my mind. I killed so many. I know they keep trying to kill me, so I will keep killing them.

While in basic training, I learned Eaters are human but with an uncommon genetic mutation. This alteration in their DNA changes them into something else entirely. They're unlike the zombies from horror movies I watched as a kid. If they bite you, you don't become one of them—you become their next meal instead. Eaters feel no pain, cold, or heat. Their teeth are always stained with blood, with bits of meat stuck between them. Usually, their lips are gone or dangling from their faces because they unknowingly chewed through them. I assume it's like getting Novocaine at the dentist and then trying to bite into something, but the numbness never goes away. They have a hyperactive metabolism, which makes them experience intense hunger. So unbearable that hunger blots out all rational thought. Even more dangerous, the creatures' saliva contains septic pathogens, which causes human flesh to start painfully rotting. After a few hours, muscles will start to cramp before everything shuts down and goes into paralysis. If they sink their teeth into you—pray you have the antibiotic. A beautiful, rare syringe filled with thick green fluid. Push the needle into the vein until the hub of the plunger touches your skin. Get every drop out of the barrel. Act quickly because you only have a few hours before paralysis sucks away your strength. The other alternative is chopping off whatever limb was bitten and leaving it behind. The Eaters will be too distracted by swarming the limb to even notice it isn't attached to you anymore, giving you some extra time to get away. I haven't seen any antibiotics since the war.

8

Crossing brick-laid alleys and cracked asphalt streets, we come upon a beautiful stone sign that reads Appalachian State University. The letters protruding out from the stone look to be unpolished copper. Continuing, we dart in and out of the shadows of old dorm rooms, looking for the library. We stop behind a big decaying wooden gazebo to take a break. We rest our backs on the termite-eaten wood.

Kyle, almost out of breath, looks up. "I'm going shopping."

Across the yard, I see why Kyle said what he said. There's a chain hanging under a torn awning holding tight to one corner of an old warped wooden sign. The sign is spinning like a top, twisting in circles with the wind. Every other spin cycle, the sign allows me to read it. The disfigured logo reads the Mast General Store.

"Kyle, it's too dangerous to go on your own," I say.

"I'll be okay, Drift. I got this. You guys find the library and meet me at the store when you're done."

Kyle heads to the Mast General Store. Seeing him slouched forward and walking lets me know he's at least learned to stay low and out of site. He reaches the store entrance. Before going inside, he puts his back against the wall next to the front door. He looks through the door and then leans back on the wall. His movement is fluid and quick. He grabs the door handle and pulls it toward him—a tiny brass bell on top of it rings. Kyle freezes for a split second. He reaches up and grabs the bell to mute the ringing, then walks inside. When the door closes, he lets go of the brass bell.

"Well… maybe he smells his candy bars in there?" Mac jokes.

I look at Mac with a grin. We both snicker. When I turn to see if Jaysi shares the exact comedic moment, her gaze is fixed on the opposite side of the courtyard. I can decipher the large iron letters from this distance. There's far more rust than paint on them now, but the sign reads Belk Library.

"That's it!" Jaysi says. Before she can run out from behind the shed, I grab her and pull her back.

"I'll go first."

I peek around the corner. It looks clear. No Eaters. No Empire patrols. It all seems a little too easy. Usually, Empire soldiers are scouring properties like this. Their absence scares me.

I sprint across the grass, bursting through the gate as I enter the courtyard—Mac, Jaysi, and Connor trail behind me, close but not quite fast enough. I focus on what's inside the fence instead of outside it. I'm almost out of breath when we all reach the front door. One by one, everyone finally makes it to the door. I grab onto the oversized handle, but the door won't open. I think about shooting off the lock, but that would draw attention from any nearby Eaters since loud noises act like dinner bells for them. We have to stay quiet if we want to stay safe. I brace myself and ram the door with my shoulder. It doesn't budge; this thing has to be reinforced steel. Well, that eliminates plan one. Maybe there's another way in. I scan the exterior for windows, but they're all at least eight feet off the ground, way out of reach from down here. This isn't going to be easy.

On the stairs sits a bronze statue of a man standing on a boulder with a metal plaque screwed into the rock. The mountaineer man has a giant beard and hat, with both his hands in the air, clenched in a fist like he just won a boxing match. I kneel next to the plaque for a moment to check it out. The plaque reads Mountaineer Spirit and Proud Heritage of Appalachian State University under the name Yosef. After reading the plaque, I jump on Yosef's back and scamper up it.

Yosef's hands, outstretched, are level with the window frame behind him so from my perch atop the statue, I have a clear view into the window.

Bracing myself, I ram the butt of Sophia through the window. The window collapses, shattering to the ground. It's louder than I want it to be. I wait a minute before leaping in. I want to make sure nothing is running toward the sound of the breaking glass. I steady myself.

I jump from the statue to the somewhat open window. My coattail rips as it catches a glass shard. The drop is not what I imagined. Even though I could see in, I assumed the floor was a foot or two under the windowpane, but it isn't. It's a five-foot drop. When I land, I land hard. The butt of Sophia, my rifle, hits the marble floor, causing an echo through the library. The sound is louder than the window breaking. Inspecting the new rip in my coat, I unlock the door.

Jaysi dashes in, trailed by Connor and Mac. I firmly close the door after them and secure the lock. The tall and thin windows allow plenty of light to enter the room. We attempt to move around the space but discover that every footstep produces a reverberating sound. Everything seems to have been left untouched since its last book was checked out. Although I'd never been here before, it looks exactly as I'd envisioned it prior to the war. Nothing was amiss or damaged. Jaysi quickly runs off to see what she can discover.

"Let's break up in pairs," I say. "Mac, you go with Connor, and I'll go with Jaysi. If we get split up, meet back at the store."

I love watching Jaysi's excitement. I don't understand why, but I enjoy it.

"I found them! History books," she says.

"Nice," I say, uninterested. I'm too busy inspecting Sophia from her hard hit on the floor. Jaysi keeps pulling out book after book. I put Sophia back over my shoulder. She falls into the standard position, the butt of the gun knocking my hind legs while the weight of the strap digs into my shoulder.

Jaysi flips through some books, choosing which ones she wants and stuffing them in my backpack. Suddenly, a book falls with a thudding sound against the marble ground. We both turn toward the source of the noise, standing still.

"We need to check it out," I whisper.

"It's just Mac and Connor dropping books."

"Will you bet your life on that?" I ask.

I hoist Sophia from my shoulder and put her in a ready position. The weight of my backpack thumps heavily against my back, reminding me of the elk meat I had hauled into Hill Top Village not too long ago. *Damn, books are heavy,* rumbles in the back of my mind. We venture closer to where the sound had originated, coming upon a room with no windows. I quickly reach into a side pocket of my bag and fish out a small flashlight, but before I can flick it on, fast-moving steps pierce the silence. *Clipity-clop, clipity-clop* reverberates throughout the library like thunder. Every muscle in my body tenses as I point my rifle in preparation for the worst. My eyes frantically scan left to right—it's only Mac and Connor sprinting toward us. Mac has a firm grip on his revolver in one hand. They must be in trouble. When they finally reach us, Mac leans forward, desperately fighting to catch his breath.

"Dar…" Panting. "Dark room. Tons of Eaters."

As we hear this, we turn to the room next to us.

"This room?" I say.

Still catching his breath, Mac points behind himself without looking, "No…back there."

Connor cuts in. "I shut the door and locked it before they could chase us. It was weird. There's like sixty Eaters crowded in the corner of this dark room. They're just staring at the wall."

I switch on the flashlight in a desperate attempt to fill the dark abyss in front of us with light. The beam of light pierces through the darkness, revealing twenty pairs of menacing eyes glaring at us from the corner. They are huddled together, synchronized in their movements, swaying back and forth like a metronome. I was so caught up in seeing something I had never seen before, my judgment was terrible. I should have shut the door immediately, but I didn't. Before too long, they come charging after us like mad demons. I don't have time to shut the door.

"Run!" I yell.

I struggle under the weight of my pack; running on the slippery marble floors is like scaling a mountain peak made of solid ice. Every movement is tense with fear, my feet sweating inside my boots. Struggling for grip against the smooth floor, I lurch around the corners, taking five small steps to my usual one. Trying my best to keep my footing. I know that if I fall now, there will be no hope of escape as twenty hungry Eaters close in on me. When we come to yet another corner, and I realize that escape is out of our reach, my instinct takes over, and I frantically scramble up one of the twelve-foot-tall bookshelves, praying desperately that the Eaters haven't learned to climb.

"Climb the bookshelves!" I scream.

Jaysi and Mac scramble desperately behind me, their feet pushing off against the books that slip and slide beneath us as we ascend higher and higher. Connor is a few shelves ahead of us but close enough for me to hear the creaking of his ascent. As we clamber higher, our feet kick off books that fall like bombs crashing loudly onto the marble floor, others smashing onto Eaters' heads before meeting the ground with a sickening thud. We push on, refusing to slow down until, finally, we reach the topmost shelf, where our faces are inches away from the metal frames of fluorescent lights that dangle from the ceiling.

"Now what?" Jaysi cries out.

The Eaters swarm around the bookshelves, bellowing their hunger and desperation. They press their foul bodies against the shelves, threatening to topple them. Our only refuge has quickly become a death trap as we realize we are stuck in the room with no escape. The shelves tremble and creak under the assault of our weight and sway dangerously with every bump from the Eaters. This motion gives me an idea.

"Follow me."

Hunched down so I don't hit my head on the fluorescent lights, I jump from one bookshelf to the other. Connor watches me as I pass him. Jaysi and Mac follow behind me until we reach the last shelf before the door. The Eaters follow below, their eyes fixated on us.

"What's your plan?" Mac yells.

"The window!"

Connor looks at the window in disbelief.

"The window?! That's your plan?! The window is like a mile away from the shelf."

We come to a stop on the very last shelf before the window. With a fierce grip, I snatch the fluorescent fixture for support.

Mac points his revolver down to shoot at the Eaters.

"Save your bullets," I tell him. "There are twenty of them. You have six bullets."

Connor leans into my face. "I won't kill myself."

"You won't have to."

I begin to rock the shelf back and forth with all my might.

"What the hell are you doing?" Connor said.

"Tryin' to make this shelf fall toward that window ledge."

Books of all sizes cascade off their shelves, like an avalanche of knowledge. *Bam!* The shelving violently rocks the other way, sending more books crashing down as they hit the marble floor. *Bam!* And again. *Bam!* And again!

"Get ready!"

The shelf shudders back and forth seven or eight times before finally succumbing to gravity and collapsing forward. We all get our footing, preparing ourselves to jump through the window. All at once we jump in the air before the shelf hits the wall, all except Connor. Connor's timing was off. Before he could leap off the shelf, it hit the wall, causing him to lose footing.

Instead of flying forward and out the window, he falls flat on the side of the shelving unit. His chin bounces off the top shelf, and his knee and shins scrape across the third and fourth shelves.

We burst through the window like a tornado, with Jaysi and Mac in front of me. Mac crashes into the statue, tumbling off the mountaineer's hat and landing hard on the unforgiving ground. Jaysi and I, however, are luckier as we tumble onto the cold ground next to the colossal boulder that serves as the monument's foundation.

"Where's Connor?" Jaysi asked.

"He lost his footing when we jumped," I said.

Connor's bag of books soars out the window, crashing down beside Jaysi. Then, Connor himself comes sailing through, landing on Mac. The impact causes Mac to collapse with a thud, spilling all his textbooks out of his bag. I hurry to help them both and quickly repack Mac's bag before holding his arm tightly as he stands back up.

"Come on. Let's get out of this area," I say as I lead everyone back to the decaying, termite-eaten gazebo. We hunker down behind it for a second to catch our breath. I knew the Eaters wouldn't chase us. The window was just too high off the ground for them.

"Holy Moly! That was crazy," Jaysi says. "I feel so alive."

Mac laughs. "Who knew Eaters couldn't climb?"

Connor sits winded and speechless. His skin is white as a ghost. A small line of blood is on the bottom of his chin from slamming it on the shelf. I say nothing to him. I'd have the same look of terror on my face if it was my first time.

"Let's go get Kyle," Mac says.

He stands up, glancing around. Slouched over, he takes off toward the Mast General Store. We follow behind him. Remembering the small bell on the door, I reach up and grab it as the door opens. We walk in slow and steady, looking for Kyle. Rusted old tin Coke, Dr Pepper, and Sprite signs hang on the wall. One even says Goo-Goo Cluster, with a picture of a flat, round chocolate sandwich with nuts in it.

"Have you seen that before?" Mac asks me.

At first, I assume he's talking about the odd-shaped candy bar but then realize he's talking about all the Eaters, huddled together in the dark rooms.

"No. I haven't. I don't think eighty to ninety Eaters would have locked themselves in a library. They don't think like that. Maybe there's something in the library the Red Empire needs to be guarded. Using Eaters that way would keep most people out. Maybe soldiers are trading Eaters to the Loco Solos—no, that makes no sense. They could be experimenting on the Eaters, and the library is their storage house."

"It didn't feel right. That's all I know," Mac replies.

Jaysi, now aware of the secrets that lie in shadows, whispers, "Shhhhhhh."

We carefully step further into the store. Every hardwood plank we step on squeaks like a built-in burglar alarm. Finally, we reach a set of stairs that descend. Going down feels as if it takes an eternity. When we arrive at the bottom floor, everything remains untouched.

It's as if we've stumbled upon an undiscovered underground treasure trove stocked with hiking gear, nutrition bars, and maps. Sure enough, Kyle has hidden away in one of the tents among the merchandise. He peeks his head out. "Whew!" he says, relaxing.

"What are you doing?" Jaysi asks.

"Hiding. The floors were squeaking so loud it sounded like the entire upstairs would collapse." I think he has fallen in some dirt until I realize he has a chocolate mustache.

"Found your candy bars, I see," Mac says as he walks around, looking at everything.

Kyle pulls out a twelve-pack of sugarcane Dr Pepper. "I found these too."

Everybody rushes over to Kyle and grabs one. Everyone except Connor, who walks over.

POP! Fizz foams out from the hole before it touches our lips. The carbonation causes us all to burp. I guess our bodies aren't used to the bubbles anymore. None of us have had anything sweet like this in a long time.

Mac grabs a few clothes off the floor.

"Did you get your shopping done?" Mac asks.

Kyle raises his backpack for all to see. Mac and I make our way over to the SmartWool sock display. I quickly take off my hiking boots and tear away the threadbare holey socks on my feet. I grab a pair of thick woolen socks with the most padding, pulling open the packaging. When I slide them on, I savor each centimeter of the new fabric as it brushes against my skin. It's like a moment of serenity.

I fling my sodden socks across the room with one big heave, creating a dark splat on the otherwise light-colored wall. I carry on shopping and find a new coat hanging on a rack. It is in better condition than the one I have on, so I take it off and trade it for the new one; finding usable winter clothes is a rarity nowadays because most shops are completely emptied or destroyed by fire. Mac then grabs a new pair of socks and tosses them to Connor; unfortunately, Connor catches them but isn't overly thrilled about it. Mac notices that Connor's right foot appears to be bothering him.

"Connor, what's wrong?" Mac asks.

Connor replies, "Nothing. I twisted my ankle jumping off that shelf."

"Shelf?" Kyle looks at Connor's ankle.

"It's nothing," he quickly replies.

Jaysi, itching to tell someone about her discovery, chimes in, "We found the library and got our books, but there were like twenty Eaters in there. They chased us, but Drift got us out."

"Eighty to ninety Eaters," Mac says, interrupting Jaysi's story.

"Well, only twenty chased us. Connor locked the other ones in a different the room."

"Eighty to ninety Eaters! Are you kidding me?" Kyle asks as he takes a slow bite off his candy bar.

I replace my light cotton shirt with a quick-drying thermal top. It's been a while since I've had decent outdoor gear. The dust from the garment rises in the air as I move. This is perfect. All the stores I've visited, even vintage or second-hand stores like Goodwill and Salvation Army, have had nothing that fit me properly or can withstand getting wet without taking forever to dry.

After I lace up a new pair of hiking boots, I put some extra socks in my backpack, along with a few extra shirts and a nice pair of gloves.

"We need to get out of town, guys," I say. "We have what we came for."

We all pick up our bags, which are now filled to the brim with textbooks, garments, and snacks. I climb the squeaky steps back to the top. As soon as I reach the top, a sound of wailing filters from the library. The dismal echo travels beyond the square, beyond the gazebo and straight into the shop doorway. It is so powerful and loud that I can feel my gut tighten.

I rush to the window, looking across the courtyard to see a patrol HUV at the library's front door. It's parked in reverse, with its back bumper just above the last step up to the entrance. Soldiers are standing around it in full battle armor. This isn't a standard patrol HUV—it looks heavier and broader. Suddenly, the HUV shakes as another roar rumbles from inside it. That sound didn't come from within the library but from inside the HUV itself! Whatever is in there seems desperate for freedom.

9

As we head out the back door, I notice blood on Connor's right boot. He's walking with a subtle limp out the door.

"You alright, Connor? You're bleeding pretty good there."

"I'm fine. Got cut on some glass."

We leave out the fire exit in the back of the store. It takes us out to a well-hidden alley. My backpack is heavy, making my hamstrings burn. Staying small and hunched over while running is difficult and doesn't help either. We pass a few stores with Kyle wanting to stop and shop again, but we have already worn out our welcome and can't carry any more weight. We keep waiting on Connor to catch up to us. At every stop we make, I feel exposed. When I see the treetops in the distance, I think about how badly I'd love to be at that tree line. A few blocks from the edge of town, we cross Stadium Drive. The gate to the stadium is unlocked. We slip inside to rest. Connor can barely walk and needs to rest. We walk through the corridor and into the large, colorful stadium. Some weeds have made their way through the turf. Thousands of seats circle the field. Giant screens cover each end zone like walls. In the middle of the field is a reality check.

"What is that?" Mac asks.

"Those are turrets and missile launchers. This is where they launch the Striker Drones."

"We should get the hell out of here," Kyle says. "This is the Red Empire's world right here."

"Abandoned, I'm sure, but I'm with you. Let's get out of here."

"Connor? Connor!" Jaysi raises her voice.

She moves to comfort him, but he topples backward and smacks his head against the ground. We jump in panic at the loud thud. His body is convulsing. Jaysi and Kyle rush to help him.

"His cut must be worse than we think," I said.

I grabbed my knife and crouch down, slicing away at his pant leg. The material is saturated with blood, sticking to my fingers. I pull out my water bottle and pour it over the wound. My stomach lurches when I see the gruesome sight—the skin around it is dark, almost eggplant-colored, and the edges of the three-inch gash are frayed like a raggedy cloth. Deep in his calf are three unmistakable tooth marks. Leaning in for a closer inspection, the smell of decaying flesh hits me like a punch, so I quickly turn my head away.

"He's bitten, and we don't have antibiotics. Shit—Eaters'll be after us soon. We need to get out of here," I say.

"We can't leave him," Jaysi cries.

"You don't get it. That bite is like blood in saltwater, and the sharks are on their way. You don't want to be here for that. Connor is gone. The paralysis has already set in from the bite. He has no more pain."

Mac asks, "He doesn't feel pain—but can he hear us? Does his brain still work?"

"I don't know. I guess," I answer.

Mac pulls his revolver out. Jaysi gasps at the sight of it. I shake my head.

"That's too loud."

Mac puts the gun away.

"What then?" he replies with a desperate tone.

I pull out my buck knife.

"You guys go ahead, and I'll catch up."

"You're gonna kill him?" Kyle says. "What, like, slit his throat or something?"

"He can't feel any pain, Kyle. He's paralyzed from head to toe. He'll just fall asleep," I say, trying to comfort them the best I can.

Tears form in Jaysi's eyes. She buries her face into Mac's chest, and Mac embraces her.

"There's got to be another way," Jaysi cries.

"The only other way is walking away," I said.

"I can't watch this." Kyle turns.

I kneel over and put my hand over Connor's eyes. Kyle starts pacing back and forth a few feet away.

"Please forgive me, Wood Chopper." That's all I ever called him before I knew his real name. I know it will make him feel better, knowing it's me. I put my blade to the soft flesh of his neck. With one fluid motion, I slice his throat. Blood starts to puddle under him. I wipe my blade off his sleeve.

"No, no, no, no!" Kyle says repeatedly, each *no* getting louder than the last.

"Pipe down, Kyle. We need to be quiet."

"You slit his throat." Kyle's voice cracks.

"He had to," Mac says defending me.

The chain-link gate rattles.

"They're here!" I say in a loud whisper.

I stand up, and we run down the stairs of the stadium. We take a left at row CC. The knee-high seats are folded up. While I'm running, I can't help but notice the seat numbers are counting backward —27, 26, 25. I can't wait for my knees to pass 3,2,1. We find ourselves at the corner of the end zone, high above the field. We stop to look back at Connor.

There have to be twenty Eaters ravaging him like hungry wolves. When the Eaters stand from their dinner, they have blood-soaked faces. Blood drips from their hands. Eaters that come late to the party lunge at the blood-soaked Eaters, gnawing at their faces. In the feeding frenzy, they can't tell the difference. One of their bloody hands touches the wall. Another Eater springs forward at the wall, hitting the concrete so hard its head splits open. Even with blood running down its face, it keeps running into the wall. Its skull goes soft, and on the last leap, it kills itself. Brain matter splatters on the white-painted cement blocks. Another Eater walks to the wall and starts sniffing it. It pushes its face against the wall as hard as it can. It licks the wall with its half-missing tongue. I try to keep Jaysi from looking, but it's too late. She stares in horror. We turn to escape, but a Striker Drone drops out of the sky before we can. It's not looking in our direction. It's facing the Eaters. It hovers a few feet from them.

"Holy Crap!" Mac says.

Like a jet engine, a loud roar echoes down the end zone corridor. We pause before the concessions and peer onto the field to see what it was. Suddenly, a sleek black HUV races onto the fifty-yard line with the distinct logo. A red triangle is outlined with yellow. Inside the triangle is a yellow silhouette of a scythe cutting wheat, circled with five stars. The top star is twice as big as the other stars. The image brings back memories of death and hate, and I feel rage brewing inside me.

The HUV zooms in from the sky, flying three feet high off the ground. The driver hits maximum afterburners to keep from smashing into the missile launchers. When the sound of the vehicle grabs the Eaters' attention, five Empire soldiers wearing rust-colored t-shirts leap out of the HUV. They aren't wearing their usual standard outfits, which is strange. Their black trousers are tucked tightly into their glossy black military boots, and each bootlace snakes up to their knees.

One of them stands behind a fifty-caliber gun, his mud-covered face and white streaks in his hair recognizable as the exact figure from Ghost Village. Are they allies? The Eaters hastily scramble down the stairs, and immediately the Empire's guns fire. Blood splatters over the blue-numbered seats. Some fall forward down the steps; others collapse backward due to the impact of the large-caliber bullets hitting their bodies. I take perverse pleasure in witnessing their demise— but am also disgusted at this alliance between the Empire and Ghost Villagers.

We slip out of the chain-link fence and return to the woods minus one. I feel safe again being on my turf. The feeling of losing Connor doesn't affect me that much. It saddens me, but I am unable to be more sensitive. The Man-O-War took that emotion from me. Watching everyone in my unit get killed seems to have dulled my emotions.

We weave through the brush, making our way to the trail. Everyone is quiet. I can understand why. They are all thinking of Connor. I can hear Jaysi sniffling from crying. My head is racing with images from the Man-O-War. Memories I buried long ago have been dragged back into the light by the sight of the Red Empire forces. I can see every face of my unit. It makes me hate the Red Empire more and more. I watched my entire unit die.

The T8 gas they released on us transformed ordinary people into those Eaters. It's hard to believe Man-O Incorporated, an American company, would invent such a devastating thing. The Red Empire used it on us, hoping it would kill everyone. When it didn't, I think they were more surprised about it than we were.

They hoped to spare their soldiers' lives by sending the T8 *robo-tics* to release the gas. Unfortunately for them, the Red Empire couldn't occupy the land when the unexpected mutation occurred. The birth of Eaters was upon us. The transformation happened to them as well. Every once in a while, I see an Eater wearing a Red

Empire uniform. I particularly enjoy killing those. The Red Empire became wise. They made a filtering implant for their soldiers. The implants keep the bloodstream uninfected. Whoever has one can walk through a gas cloud without being affected. The implant is the same size as the head of a toothbrush and is in the left shoulder. I know this because I cut one out of a soldier once who no longer needed his. The minute I did, the small green light on the implant turned off, so I assumed the internal body heat kept it charged. Once the Red Empire soldiers received their implants, all hell broke loose.

They sent T8s out by the thousands with their troops to follow.

No. With Eaters swarming everywhere, the Red Empire will have to wait before they can move in. There are no implants to repel the Eaters. That's why units are small and sparsely placed around the city. I'm sure they're hopeful the Eaters will kill all of us and starve themselves. Too bad the Eaters are lasting longer than expected.

The Red Empire sees things one way, their way. The merger started with Russia, China, and North Korea. Nations coined them the Red Empire because all their flags had one dominating theme: the color red. Germany, Syria, and Cuba followed. Other smaller countries joined. They were smart enough to get in with the big dogs before the big dogs took them over.

With pockets deeper than the Grand Canyon, their technology grew faster than ours. They have the most remarkable minds working around the clock creating advanced weapons, computers, and everything in between, leaving us outdated. Still, we tried to hang on to the belief that we were an almighty power to be reckoned with until the Red Empire proved us wrong. There are always two sides to every story. We say they attacked us because they wanted world domination for total control. The Red Empire said they attacked us for forcing our political beliefs on them. Both reasons were probably right.

10

On the way back, no one speaks a word. We all walk with heavy feet, our eyes vacant, and bowed heads, lost in our thoughts. I wonder if Jaysi will document this experience in her records. Forever known as the guy who killed the Wood Chopper from Hill Top Village. Will she date it? Will she write his birthday, add a dash, then the date I killed him?

Who cares, I tell myself. I shake off the thought of trying to keep track of the date. Who needs to know what day it is out here? Not me. All I need to know is day or night; other knowledge doesn't matter. I tried to keep up with dates for a while, even attempting to remember my birthday, but that stopped after the war placed me on the front lines when I was fifteen. I'm probably nineteen or twenty now. Who knows. You lose track of everything over the winter seasons. Even though the days are short, the darkness, cold, and loneliness make them slow and tedious. I used to carve lines with my knife into an oak tree to keep up, but it made me more depressed. Each line represented a month of living while everything and everyone I lived for was gone. I decided these were days I wanted to forget, not keep track of, so I stopped. Birthdays are memories best left forgotten. Now, every day I'm given is my birthday.

The faces of the Red Empire soldiers have been etched in my memory. They felt so sure of themselves as they fired upon the Eaters in that stadium. I bet they laughed while they shot at my former unit during the war too. I'd always believed war was meant for fathers and soldiers, not children. They took my childhood when they trained me to be a killer. Or maybe Serge was right. I was born to be a soldier.

I wasn't always as calloused and numb as I am now. The first time I gazed upon the devastation of war, I was overcome with tears. Ash covered my face from the still-burning and smoldering buildings and HUVs. When the tears started to roll down my cheeks, the white ash on my face turned dark gray. Even at thirteen, I was too much of a "man" to sniffle and wipe my face but still too much of a boy not to cry.

"SOLDIERS DON'T CRY, BOY!" Serge yelled an inch from my face. This time, he spared me the accompaniment of his spit. He had none to give. None of us did. After days of marching and breathing in smoke and ash, we were just too worn out and dehydrated. Plus, I knew he felt the same feelings I did. Watching your homeland turn into rubble isn't an easy thing to swallow. So, my response to him was soft and quiet.

"Sir, yes, sir."

We were marching through small towns that looked identical to all our own small towns. Not some foreign land or unfamiliar territory. Hometowns. It was a war at our doorsteps, in our backyards. As we made our way through the cities, nobody waved miniature American flags from their father's shoulders. No old veterans saluted us.

We saw mothers lying beside their children, decaying right alongside each other. Inside the Mini-HUVs were mummified families and burnt stuffed animals still clutched in babies' hands. Skeletons of drivers buckled into their seats, still looking for a way out of town. Everywhere I looked, buildings were destroyed, fires were burning, and smoke was rising from the rubble. It was hard to imagine anything surviving in such a disaster zone. The Red Empire's intervention with our technology had left us helpless, like they'd cut off our lifelines, hacking in and stopping all HUV flights before they invaded us. When the HUVs dropped from the sky, it was like witnessing metal raining from above, as some burst into flames while others exploded on impact. Some just landed with a giant thud. Now, they were the only ones with hovering vehicles while we marched like a third world country hanging on to hope that we could rebuild ourselves.

The bullets and bombs ravaged buildings, leaving gaping holes. Piles of shattered glass and bricks littered the foundations of the buildings. Missing walls of apartments and office buildings allowed us to see into their charcoaled worlds. It's a hard thing to lay eyes on and an even more challenging thing to forget.

My unit had become like family to me during the war, but they were taken from me one by one. Now Stick's and Connor's faces and the sensation of cutting his throat with my blade are added to the memories in my head. Will Jaysi be next? Can I keep living if her death is etched in my memory?

Hearing villager voices in the distance brings me back to reality. Walking into the village and seeing it still standing is a breath of fresh air. The first thing we do is go to the second cabin to grab something to eat. Dropping those bags of books and new clothes is a relief. We find seats behind piping hot bowls of soup. We rip the loaf of bread apart and pass it around. It reminds me of how the Eaters tore Connor apart. I can tell Jaysi is thinking the same thing. She pushes the hot soup forward and sits back in her chair. I finish my soup and then ask if she is eating hers. She has both her arms crossed as if she's holding her stomach from spilling out. She just shakes her head no. I slide her bowl in front of me. I eat hers, which is now cooler and easier to eat than mine was.

"How can you eat?" she asks.

"I've seen it all. I've been through a lot worse than that. Hunger pains. That's worse."

Jaysi—in shock I guess—stands and paces back and forth.

"I'm the Keeper, right! I need to write this all down! We have to document what happened to Connor. What if we die tonight? Who will tell his story? The ability not to walk after he was bit needs to be known. The Eaters were able to hunt the rotting flesh. You know these things, but we don't. When you leave us, we need to know these things."

The door opens, and Connor's brother walks in. He's barely across the threshold before he asks, "Where's Connor?"

Mac stands. He answers slow and soft. "He didn't make it, Woody."

The woodchopper takes a step into the cabin but stops. He puts his hand on the doorframe and slouches over. Tears form in the corners of his eyes. He does his best to hold them back, but the tears win. As they fall, he wipes his eyes with his calloused hands and smears tears across his cheeks.

"How did he die?"

Jaysi stands and walks over to him. "Woody, I'll write it all in the journal so that you can read it later."

He stands from his slouch.

"Read it later? Just tell me how he died?"

Mac answers before anyone else speaks. "Eaters."

Mac didn't want someone else to speak up first saying I slit his throat and left him dead. We all decided together, and it was true. Eaters killed him.

"I hope those bastards choked on him," Woody mumbles.

Kyle stops eating long enough to tell a satisfying tale. I guess he figures it would cheer Woody up.

"Even better. A Red Empire Striker Drone found the herd of Eaters. Five minutes later, a patrol unit showed up in their HUV and shot so many bullets into the Eaters. They killed all of 'em."

Kyle held up his hands while he told the story, pretending to shoot a machine gun. As he told the story, he forced wind through-hardened lips, doing his best machine gun impression. *Pshhh, pshhh, pshhh.*

Mac puts his hand on Kyle's shoulder and squeezes it. I can tell the story didn't make the woodchopper feel any better. He drops his head lower than his shoulders and walks out. Jaysi turns and sits back down.

"Are you going to say I slit his throat in the archives?" I ask.

Mac sits back down. "We should leave that out."

I respond, "No way. I killed him. I didn't want the last thing he saw to be an Eater eating his intestines. I did it for Connor's own good."

Jaysi drops her head. "Yes… When someone else gets stuck in that position, they need to know that is an option. They need to know how we survived so they can survive."

"You must write 'we,' Jaysi, 'we' slit his throat, so no one gets blamed," Mac says.

"I'll write 'we,'" she responds. "It's my fault anyways. I'm the one that insisted we go to town for those stupid books."

"What's done is done. It's no one's fault," Mac said.

Kyle's spoon clatters against the bottom of his bowl. He sets the bowl on the table and wipes his mouth with his sleeve. He leans over and pulls a Dr Pepper from his bag and pops the top. It foams as he takes a large gulp.

"'We' it is!" he says.

Once our stomachs are full, we lug the heavy bags of books to cabin one, where Jaysi is organizing her library. I search through my bag and pull out a book about American history, another about world history, and one detailing the life of John Adams. What an interesting hairdo, I think to myself, picturing how it would look on me. After unpacking my bag, I move on to Connor's—clearly, he had been preparing for the long haul. The first two books I pluck out are Identifying Trees of North America and Edible Plants of North America. Obviously, he was thinking ahead—these titles would help the villagers with their daily lives. As I take out these books, my admiration for Connor grows.

How To Build A Log Cabin.

This book stops me. I can't help but smile. I take the book and walk out of the room, leaving Mac and Jaysi to file their new library books.

Kyle is still in cabin number two. He didn't grab any books in the library. Just winter clothes and two super light aluminum cooking pots. I'm sure he thought he could impress Isabella with them.

The events of the last four days race through my mind as I walk to the barn. When I see Woody, he is in the process of splitting a massive log with an ax. His swings are so powerful that bits of wood fly farther than usual. It is obvious that this is his way of dealing with stress. As he feels me approach, he stops and slowly turns toward me, gripping the ax handle tightly and his knuckles turning white. I'm thinking he might use it on me for a second until he releases his grip and sits down on the log. I don't know why I chose to give him this book; I wanted to keep my distance from everyone in town, but I recognized what it was like to lose a brother—an entire unit of brothers.

I hand the book to him, and he's immediately drawn to the image on the front cover. It shows an ax lodged between a piece of wood, a log cabin in the background with smoke coming out from the chimney. He brushes away tears with his hands before accepting the book. With extreme care, he flips through it, taking in all of the illustrations that explain how to construct a log cabin—from selecting the right tree to notching the wood.

"Connor got this book for both of you," I tell Woody as he turns through the pages. When he closes it up again, there's a tiny dot of red blood on the front, and he drags his thumb across it softly.

"Is that Connor's?" he asks.

"It is."

He sets the book on top of a tree stump, which serves as an impromptu table.

"Thanks, Drift."

With an ax in hand, he starts to whack at the log again, this time with a vengeance. He is trying to use this tree-chopping activity to relieve his pain. I back away, letting him have some space, and go to my stall, where I put my backpack on my blanket.

My feet are sore. The new hiking boots are too stiff. I still have my old pair. I tied their laces together and slung them over my shoulder. Two pairs of boots out here are a rarity. I'll break in the new ones eventually. I'll try to keep my blisters to a minimum by trading them out occasionally. Another rarity. Being able to break them in slowly.

I fall asleep. A full belly and a soft place to land are welcoming.

11

Sitting up from the best night's sleep I've had in a while, I wipe the sleep from my eyes. A yawn comes as I lace up my old boots. I am sparing my feet the torture of the new hard leather boots today. Like usual, I put Sophia over my shoulder and head out of the barn. I look down at Woody as I am leaving. He's passed out next to the almost-disintegrated log. A twelve-foot-long log was turned to wood chips by one guy overnight. I hope I never fall under his ax. I hit the dining cabin for a bit of grub. Everyone is involved in doing something. Each villager has chores they take pride in doing. My task comes later today. It's my watch tonight. After breakfast, I'm going back to the barn to clean Sophia. I want her in tip-top shape for this evening.

The day goes by quickly. Winter days never go by this fast. I've eaten two meals. I'm dry, and I'm prepared for watch duty tonight. I throw Sophia over my shoulder and walk to where the guys keeping watch are. I tap one on the shoulder and relieve him of his duties.

"Anything out of the ordinary?" I ask as he walks off.

"A flock of geese flew by."

I gaze up at the night sky like they were still there. The crew gathers around me to hear instructions on their tasks. Taking my position on top of cabin one, I settle down in the mix of branches, mud, and leaves: the perfect ingredients for my favorite camouflage. The scene in before me is breathtaking. The reds and pinks of the setting sun color everything around for miles. It's a view I experience often, but it never fails to give me pause. If only Jaysi were here with me, she would love this.

After a few minutes, I reach out and put some snow in my mouth to lessen the steam when I exhale. The village below continues with its daily routines. The ones that that know I'm up here keep looking up at me.

I think of Woody as I scan the tree line with a pair of binoculars. They were issued to me in basic training. Inside the rubber eyecups of my binoculars, a small digital reading of wind speed, distance, and trajectory show up. I enjoy not having to think too much when holding a tool like this. Binoculars make it easier. I still have to rely on my instincts and gut feelings. I don't need the binoculars for every shot. I can calculate the wind with other instruments that nature provides. Falling leaves, swaying branches, or half-burned flags popping in the wind.

For the hundredth time, I scan the tree line. Something catches my attention. A head bouncing up and down. Someone is running. The hair on their head has white streaks like the boy on the fifty-caliber machine gun and the scavengers that killed Stick. He is running with a slouch, trying to stay undetected. He isn't just passing by Hill Top Village. He is up to no good. Pinpointing his next position, I set the binoculars down and pick up my rifle. I put him in my crosshairs. It magnifies his head better than the binoculars. My eyes focus on the cracking mud that coats his face. His sky-blue eyes stand out against the white mud. He hurriedly passes a few trees, then vanishes behind a hut. I keep the gun moving at the rate he is running, expecting him to emerge from the other side. When he doesn't, I stop and study the area with my scope. Scanning back and forth, he seems to have vanished from sight. A girl walks out of the hut. The same girl that's always lying in her hammock while the smoke in her hut smolders. She picks up some old firewood that is stacked by the entrance. In seconds, he races out of the forest and grabs the girl. Before she can scream, he covers her mouth with his hand. With the other, he holds a knife up to her throat. She feels the blade and stops struggling. He guides her to the tree line behind her hut. I can see a bloodline where the blade's edge touches her skin. The dried mud on his face cracks a little more as he smiles. I know he thinks he got away. Right before he takes his last step into the woods… *Peeuwooooooo.* The bullet hits his forehead so hard his neck snaps backward. Still holding the girl, they both fall to the ground. She lands on top of his lifeless body. She struggles to get out of his limp embrace. She frees herself and stands, looking down to see that it is one of the mud-faced boys. The white mud turns a muted pink as the blood trickles down his face from his forehead, leaving a trail that leads all the way to his left earlobe. The sound of her screams mixed with the gunshots send terror through the village. She slips and slides through the muddy slush as she makes her way back into the common space, continually turning her head to look behind her. A white handprint remains above her mouth, a reminder of what could have happened.

I pull back the deadbolt, and the used bullet flies out of the chamber; then I quickly push the deadbolt forward, loading a new one. Smoke rises from my rifle, and I take in a deep breath of the gunpowder. The smell always sends a rush of adrenaline through me.

Number One, the village leader, screams to all the villagers. "Here, here!" He is waving them into the false security of the log cabin. They race toward it while eight other Ghost Villagers burst from the woods. I take out three more before they have a chance to realize what's happening. I remind myself I only have one more bullet left in the magazine before switching to a new one. Sophia holds five shots per magazine, and I have two magazines. I usually keep one bullet in the chamber, but I decided not to this time. Maybe it was laziness, or maybe I had grown too comfortable being here. My final shot goes through the neck of the furthest attacker.

I eject the magazine from my rifle and insert the new one. The empty mag slides off the cabin's A-frame and plops down at the feet of Number One. His attention diverted, he gets tackled by a Ghost Villager and thrown backward onto the porch beam. After getting to his feet, Number One takes a few swings in retaliation, connecting with a haymaker. The Ghost Villager falls to the ground, unconscious. Number One walks back onto the porch and grabs the spear we pulled out of Stick. I left it leaning against the doorway so they could remember to always be on their guard. With both hands on the spear, Number One leaps off the porch's top step and into the air. He thrusts the spear with all his might into the chest of a Ghost Villager. It's something I never thought I'd see: a Hill Top Villager killing another human being.

Number Two is running as fast as he can, which isn't fast considering his weight. An attacker wielding a wooden baseball bat is chasing him. Nails have been hammered through the thick part of the wood. The sharp pointy ends stick out in every direction. It's one of the scariest weapons I've seen other than a Striker Drone. Lifting the bat high above his head, he readies the bat to come down like a hammer on Number Two's head. Number Two trips in the thick mud and falls. The attacker swings and misses. Number Two is out of breath and exhausted. He crawls in the mud until he gives up and turns on his back. He struggles to open his right eye, the part of his face not covered with dry mud. As the attacker repositions for the final blow, I put a bullet in his head. Brain matter and skull fragments rain down on Number Two. Some of it lands in his screaming mouth. He spits and gags. He rolls to his stomach and vomits.

At that moment, Woody comes out of the barn with his ax. I don't know if he knows it's a Ghost Village attack or even cares. He's just ready to fight somebody or something. A Ghost Villager runs toward Woody, holding the food he stole. He is trying to run without the movement of swinging his arms. I watch as Woody turns his ax to the flat metal side. He connects with the thief so hard that his feet fly in the air, and his head hits the ground. I see Woody lift his ax. He is about to drop on the thief, but a scream belts out from the opposite direction. I never see if Woody finishes the job, but I assume he did. I turn my scope to the screams. Another Ghost Villager is sprinting toward the tree line. He's the last of the raiders.

I get a shot off and the bullet catches him in the back of his thigh. He collapses onto the muddy ground, the crowbar he was holding slipping away from his grip. It flips a few times in the air before landing in the bushes. Through my scope, I can see him get to his feet, his gaze directed toward me like he knew exactly where I was.

The Ghost Villager moves his finger from one side of his throat to the other, a warning gesture that he knew I would recognize. "Not today," I think to myself, pulling the trigger. The bullet causes him to tumble backward, his head burrowing into the mud. His knees are awkwardly bent, while his feet end up underneath his body.

The entire village is rushing toward the same cabin I'm lying on. Bodies lie scattered on the ground, but people jump over them in an effort to reach it. Mac looks up at me and says reassuringly, "Everyone is alive." I stand my ground for another four hours as muffled voices drift through the ceiling from below. In my mind, I can hear Jaysi saying: "I'm the Keeper, and we need full details for the archives."

I release my box magazine. I put a bullet in the chamber while I reload just in case I need to get a quick shot off. It's hard to fathom that we have endured wars like World War III, Man-O-War, Eaters, T8s, and Striker Drones just to come to this: killing each other. If the Ghost Villagers are allies of the Red Empire, why don't they just mow these Hill Top Villagers down with machines? What is the purpose of using sticks and spears? Maybe they need the villagers alive for some reason. These thoughts vanish as soon as they come: all that matters now is not dying.

12

As I enter the cabin, Number One, Two, Jaysi, Mac, and Kyle are gathered around the table. Mud covers them from head to toe. The other Hill Top Villagers have already left the cabin. Jaysi walks into the kitchen and brings out a steaming bowl of soup and a piece of freshly torn bread, which she places in front of me. The way they are looking at me they all have something to say, but none of them speak. Mac finally breaks the silence.

"That was the most amazing display of shooting I've ever seen."

His words make it easier for Number One to cut in. "We owe you a debt of gratitude. We would be dead if you weren't here. Thank you!"

"Thank you? I'm just doing my job. I have two weeks left, and then I'm going—and they didn't want you dead. They wanted you all alive."

Number Two says, "You can't leave now! You killed all those men out there! They'll be back, looking for revenge. You don't get a single bullet until you see this through."

"Nonsense!" Number One says. "We told Drift two months. I shook on it, and that's that. I will not go back on my word."

"Your pride, Number One, will get us all killed… We must send Drift to the Ghost Village while he is on our clock. He must wipe out the entire Ghost Village population."

"I am here to protect you. Not fight a war and die for you. I won't assassinate a whole village for your sake. I've served my country already! I'll serve your needs. I'll protect the village for two weeks. After that, I'm gone."

"Maybe we should move," Mac says. Everyone at the table seems uneasy. I can tell they are used to the comforts here, which is another sign of weakness. Not being able to walk away at any moment.

"Everything we have is here. We've worked too hard making this place a home," Number Two says.

"Neither will solve our problem," Number One says.

"We should negotiate then," Number Two says.

Number One lifts his hand and starts to rub the corners of his mouth, then runs both of his hands through his hair. The restlessness is noticeable, and so is his concern.

"Drift says they want us alive. Won't we be walking right into their trap? Why do they want us alive is the real question here?" he asks.

"I'll go!" Kyle says.

Jaysi jumps up. "You? You can't go. They'll just kill you! You don't know the first rule of negotiating. We need an elected official to take the terms. That's how it should be."

I find an opening between the conversation to speak.

"We saw a Ghost Villager with the Red Empire soldiers in the city. I don't think he's some random rogue. He was shooting their .50 cal… That means he's authorized to shoot Red Empire weapons. The gun wouldn't have fired if not. His DNA is in their system. When we ran out of ammo during the war, we picked up their weapons to use them, but they wouldn't fire. There has to be a partnership between them and the Red Empire. Why? Why would a massive force need a small village? No, this won't be an easy walk-in and walk-out. I always thought Ghost Villagers were a bunch of Loco Solos. I avoided them at all costs. Why would they keep Eaters locked up but not eat 'em? It doesn't make sense. They partnered with the Red Empire for a reason. There's something bigger here we aren't seeing. Did you know the Ghost Villagers before the attacks?"

"We knew a few of the kids early on," Mac says. "Some even lived with us before moving over there. Once that old man became the leader, it all changed. They became more alpha. More reckless. We had to cut ties with 'em."

"How long ago was that?" I ask.

"Years ago."

"So should we negotiate with them or not?" Number Two asks.

"This is your village. That has to be your call. The village should take a vote. Whatever the outcome. Sophia is not the deciding factor."

Number Two gives me a puzzled look. "Who is Sophia?"

I pat my rifle. "It's my gun."

"If we all agree to negotiate, I'll go," Number One insists.

"Nonsense. You should never send the president into harm's way. This job is mine," Number Two says as he stands. "When do we leave?"

In my short time here, I never thought he would put himself in harm's way like this. Maybe he wants revenge or to redeem himself for being so cowardly. I stand up to see if I can call his bluff.

"Right now, if you'd like."

Number Two walks around the table, still wet, caked with mud and bone fragments sprinkled on top.

"I shall bathe first and put on clean attire. Then, I will be ready to go."

"Before you do. Let me ask you what we are asking of them, and what are we offering them?" I ask.

"We're going to ask them to stop raiding us and taking people."

"Ok. Say they do agree to stop. What are you offering them?"

"Vegetables, cabin construction, bullets. You know, those kinds of things."

"If you offer him those bullets. You will all be dead. They can't find out about the bullets," I say.

"Ok. No bullets—let's just find out what they want. Then we'll start the peace treaty," Number Two says.

I exit the log cabin and walk down the stairs. I lean over to pick up the box magazine that slid off the roof during the attack. I take it back to Mac's workstation and clean it, reloading it with the five allotted bullets. I put about fifty rounds of bullets in my pouch. I decide, since I have time to rest, to take off my boots. I pull my wet socks off. I dig through my bag and pull out a new pair of *SmartWool* socks. I don't put them on right away. I let my feet air out. Wiggling my toes without constriction feels therapeutic.

Kyle comes into the barn. He hands me what looks to be a candy bar.

"There was a box of these things in town. I brought 'em all back. It says energy bar on it. You might need to power up out there."

I grab it from him and thank him. The wrapper is light blue with a man dangling from a rock. The white words that sit inside a red rectangle box on the wrapper read *Clif Bar*. Kyle made sure I knew it was chocolate-chip flavor. Seeing the cliff on the wrapper has got me thinking.

"Do you know what the terrain is like around their village?" I ask.

He answers but not in a confident tone of voice.

"Well…ah…there aren't any trees on one side. Just huge rocks peeking out of tall, brown grass. I'm sure that's how I remember it."

I refill my water bottle and prep my gear once again.

"I'll figure it out when I get there," I say.

I was hoping to know because I like to keep myself busy while I walk by, preparing my camouflage. Plus, I don't want to have long conversations with Number Two during the hike.

Jaysi walks in. "Sorry."

"For what?"

"You're always asked to do all these dangerous things. It doesn't seem fair."

"Nothing's ever fair for me."

"Since you've shown up, I have written more entries in the log than my entire time as the Keeper. You sure know how to make history, don't ya," Jaysi says.

Mac walks in next.

"Number Two is on the porch, waiting. I gave him some of those wool socks we scored from the general store. Hopefully, he won't complain as much about the hike. You'll have to stop a lot. The farthest I've ever seen him walk is from cabin one to cabin two for meals."

I laugh a little. *Am I getting in too close?* It seems like I'm getting comfortable. I don't want any more friends to die around me, so *this is it.* If all goes right, when we return from this trip, they won't need my services anymore. I'll leave this place behind with my bullets.

After I pack my bag, I put on the *SmartWool* socks and then strap on my old boots. Since we're walking, I figure I'll save my feet the agony of blisters. I put my backpack on and then throw Sophia over my shoulder. Everyone follows me out of the barn. Number Two is standing on the porch, glowing with pride. He is in a wrinkle-free, somewhat dusty old suit with his pant legs tucked into his socks. His shoes are shiny. He looks at me.

"I am representing Hill Top Village. Dressed to impress, you might say."

"You will hike in those shoes. Why not wear boots and then when we get there you can change?" I ask.

"Carry them? Yes. Yes, I guess you're right."

He goes back inside. Kyle pats my back and wishes me luck and then goes back to the barn. Woody walks out holding two shovels. I'm assuming they'll dig a large grave for all the dead bodies. With any luck, they won't add any more to the pile by the end of the day.

13

Number Two is barely keeping pace, panting heavily beside me. A day-and-a-half hike has taken three days. I know we're close when the stench of rotting flesh drifts through the air.

"Oh! What's that smell?" Number Two asks.

"Remember when you asked me how I didn't know about this place? Well, this is why. I thought they were Loco Solos."

I kneel behind an evergreen bush and glance over the terrain, looking for my best position. I know where I want to be. It looks like it'll be a twenty-minute walk from here. By the time I get there, the sun will be at a perfect height if I have to take a shot at them. They'll be looking right into the sun when they look up at me. The sun will be on my side for at least thirty minutes once I get there.

"Where will you be?" asked Number Two.

I never give away my position. If this guy gets tortured, he will give me up in a heartbeat. I just answer him as vaguely as possible.

"Close. Give me twenty minutes before you walk into the village. I need to get to my vantage point first… twenty minutes, ok?"

"Twenty minutes. Got it."

I take fifteen minutes to reach the spot. Quicker than expected, which is great. I find the best vantage point I can. Once I settle in,

I look through my binoculars. My view is perfect. The sun is at my back and not blinding me.

Number Two starts to walk into Ghost Village, slow and careful. His pant legs are free from his socks, and his shining penny loafers are back on. He walks at attention, holding a stick with a white T-shirt tied to it. The Ghost Villagers walk over to him one at a time.

I scan the village with my binoculars. A few skinny, rectangular shacks and two large cages stand outside a large cabin. The metal wheels on the cages are so rusted that they appear to be melting into the mud. One cage has twenty Eaters, and as villagers walk past, bloody, and broken arms reach through the bars of the Eater's cage, begging for their flesh. The second cage is filled with regular humans, unturned. A village capturing and holding this many humans is a first for me. Are they feeding them to the Eaters, or is there another purpose?

The village backs up to a hundred-year-old train track. I notice two entrances to the village; each has a fire burning. This seems more tactical than anything else, a way to keep the stench of the Eaters down rather than to keep warm. The scenery on each side of the village is rugged and mountainous. The steep slopes are perfect protection for them. I'm on the west side. They can't climb so quickly to me if I'm spotted. It buys me time for an escape if they come looking.

Number Two continues toward the large cabin. Ghost Villagers start to follow behind him, each of them holding homemade weapons. Mostly teenage boys and a few young men. There are no girls. They start to caw in unison, sounding like crows. A noise I can even hear up here. I'm assuming this is a way for them to welcome Number Two or tell the other villagers to beware of danger. While they caw, a young man steps forward. He looks strong. His body is toned and taut, and he has no shirt, even during winter. This may be how they prove their manhood. The crowing turns into something else. I strain to hear and make out the new chant. It could be "moose" or "noose." When I turn my ear toward the sound, I hear the words "Roos, Roos." His name must be Roos. He looks to be my age or maybe a couple years older. The mud on their faces makes it difficult to judge their exact ages.

When Roos strides toward Number Two, a cruel smile twists his lips. He circles Number Two twice, lightly brushing his hair with each pass. He then pretends to brush dirt from Number Two's shoulder. Finally, Roos stops in front of him and is face to face with Number Two, who is trembling. Roos reaches out and fixes the collar of Number Two before delivering a sharp blow to his stomach. His malicious laughter echoes as he walks behind Number Two and kicks the back of his right knee, sending him down into the muddy soil. His chubby knees sink deep in the mud. Roos walks in front of him again, grabbing the stick that holds the white flag from him. Number Two struggles to keep hold of it, but Roos is too powerful. As I watch, my finger twitches against my trigger while I ask myself again—should I shoot?

Roos pretends the stick is a spear and takes a few steps before throwing it into the mud. The white T-shirt is now anything but white. He then walks back toward Number Two, finger-wagging from side to side. Even at this distance, I know that means no. Roos turns and walks toward the cabin. Was there another leader in there? Why didn't he invite Number Two inside? And where was the old man that everyone had been talking about?

Roos comes running out of the cabin. This time, his hands aren't empty. He is holding a machete. I can't react fast enough. Roos doesn't hesitate or slow down. He swings the blade as hard as he can. He connects with Number Two's neck. His head rolls a few yards away before stopping in the thick mud. His body falls like a freshly cut tree.

Peeuwoooooo. Peeuwooooo. Peeuwoooooo. I send three bullets into the crowd, dropping three villagers. I aim for Roos, but the scattering crowd gets in my way. At least the bullets aren't wasted. *Peeuwoooooo. Peeuwoooooo. Peeuwoooooo.* I empty the rest of my magazine. I drop the spent magazine, insert the new one as fast as possible, and put the empty magazine in my pouch.

Ghost Village wouldn't have even known I was there if I didn't shoot, but I did. I gave Number Two my word that Sophia and I would be there for him. Even if he's dead. I couldn't face Jaysi, knowing I did nothing.

Most of the villagers have taken cover. One person is lying behind a tree stump, only showing me about three inches of his forehead. I shoot, and he instantly becomes still. Immediately after, another villager attempts to escape by running from one shack to another. I pull the trigger. The force from the bullet causes him to fall on his side, face-planting in the mud. With one usable arm, he does his best to belly crawl to cover. No need to waste another bullet on him because he'll be dead by the time the sun sets. I scan the village. There's another villager lying under the farthest shack. I can barely make him out, but I know he's there. His silhouette gives him away. As I point my weapon, the entire shack trembles, and quivers. Something huge is inside, trying to break free. The same earsplitting roar I heard at the library in town fills the air. The shack is about to fall apart from the shaking.

Just as I am about to fire off a shot at the shack, a whizzing sound zooms past my ear. Thud! Pebbles go flying from the mountainside behind me. After that, the noise from the rifle echoes.

I have the sun to my back, blinding whoever is shooting at me. I quickly roll away from the rock, giving me shelter, and sprint toward the next one. Another bullet whizzes past me, this one inches from my kneecap. I keep running from rock to rock until I'm just three feet from the tree line. A shot hits my pack, causing it to swing around and making me stumble a bit as I dive headfirst behind the safety of a hemlock tree. *Thwack!* Its bark splinters under the impact of another bullet. I hear the rifle shot after the thwack.

I take off, sprinting deep into the woods. My breaths coming out in ragged gasps as I try to steady my pace. My escape plan involves following the tree line along the clearing, giving me a clear view of anyone approaching from that direction. Finally out of sight, I stop to catch my breath and reload. The adrenaline pumps hard through my veins, and every sound makes me jump. Despite this, something deep within me tells me to keep going, to stay alive.

A Red Empire patrol HUV drops down from overhead, its engine shifting from a deep rumble to a high-pitched screech as the thrusters are reversed. They must have their infrared heat detection on. I can feel the heat from the thrusters. I hear one word from over the engine: "Gun!" The soldier on the bow of the HUV fires, but it's not bullets that come my way: it's a heavy black net with weights. I dive and roll down a hill into an old drainage ditch. The net opens like a spider web. It catches on a tree above me, causing sparks to fly everywhere. Luckily, I'm spared from its electrical embrace.

I contemplate climbing inside the concrete culvert and hiding. Maybe wherever it came out was a safer place than this, or perhaps it's a dead end. With that conclusion, I stay the course and run deeper into the woods. I hear the thrusters of the HUV turn back to the low tone. I know they are moving forward along the clearing.

Round after round, bullets fly above my head from the patrol HUV. Being in this ditch, I'm below the shots, but I hear them whizzing above my head, splintering snow-covered branches. The snow falls like a blizzard all around me. Abruptly, the gunfire stops. The woods' thickness makes it too difficult for the HUV to advance. It's just too bulky of a vehicle to move around. Their only option is to pursue me on foot or send in a Striker Drone and take the entire area out. I don't wait around to see what they decide.

I take off in the opposite direction of the HUV, keeping a steady pace using rhythmic breathing. Inhaling every three steps and exhaling every two. If the HUV gains altitude, its infrared will pick me up. But as long as they stay low, it will only pick up what's below them.

"Caw-caw… Caw-caw…"

Ghost Villagers are in front of me! How? Did I run in circles or something? No, I couldn't have. I look around, grabbing low-growing moss, ferns, and mud and plastering them on my skin and my already camouflaged jacket until I blend with the surroundings. A moss-covered hollow log becomes my hiding place. I stick Sophia in first, then squeeze myself in. It's tight, almost too tight. There is just enough space for my stomach to expand and get air into my lungs. With my right hand, I rake leaves over the hole in the log. A hole no bigger than the size of my fist allows a small ray of daylight to enter the log. The mud on my face keeps the sun from reflecting off my skin.

Their steps are close now. Their footsteps say there are four or five of them. I'm soaked. The mud I put all over me has me waterlogged. The dampness inside the log doesn't help either.

"Shooter Boy. I know you're here, Shooter Boy," Roos says in a playful whisper. I wish I had taken a high position instead of this log. I could have taken a few more of these assholes out, but it's too late now. Besides, if Roos were a sharpshooter, he would predict that move. I'm committed to where I lie now. I take a deep breath and exhale slow and steady to make sure my stomach doesn't lift or sink.

Someone's foot is stepping over the log. As it comes down, it brushes the log. Flakes of dirt and bark fall into the hole. I close my eye, but it is too late. A few flakes get in my eye. *Wipe it and die,* I tell myself. Everything in my body is telling my hand not to wipe my eye. I want to move my head just in case he steps on it, but I remain still.

With his next step, I feel his heel brush the log.

"I can smell you, Shooter Boy," Roos says as the steps become more distant; his voice softens until it is no longer present.

I lie there for another hour, my eye tearing from the debris in it. I blink repeatedly in hopes that whatever is in my eye will come out. I'm so constricted. My brain tells me to wipe it, but I don't. Finally, I feel it's safe. I roll out of the log and immediately rub my eye.

They're going to be coming for Hill Top, and they are way ahead of me.

14

Cabin one and the barn are the only structures left standing. Flames climb the walls of the dining cabin. Pops and cracks come from inside the cabin as the fire consumes the dry wood and everything in it. The fire is feasting. The heat is unbearable. Ash falls slowly like snow on my face and shoulders. It's a matter of time before it collapses. In front of the cabin are a few dead bodies in the mud. When there's trouble, everyone runs to the dining cabin. Everyone.

"Jaysi!" I scream.

I sprint to cabin one, where Jaysi's bedroom and library are. When I walk inside, I notice there is no heat. White ash swirls around the fireplace. No sign of Jaysi, Number One, or Mac. I work my way down the hall to Jaysi's room. The door is closed. I put my fingers on the door handle. I want to scream her name. I want to know if she is safe behind this door, but I keep quiet. Someone else could be in there. I don't want to lose my element of surprise. I twist the handle and push the door open. I lift Sophia up and put her in a ready shooting position. Inside, the room has an orange glow. I can see the blaze from the other cabin through the window. I check the bathroom, behind the door, and the makeshift library, which was once a closet. No one is here.

I rush out of the room. Sophia's harness catches the doorknob jerking me back. Before I can unlatch it, an Eater runs toward me from down the hall. Its left shoulder is rubbing against the wall, almost like it can't stand upright. His shoulder hits hanging pictures, each dropping to the ground like glass bombs. He picks up speed. Faster and faster. Frames falling to the floor. I slide the harness strap off my shoulder. Sophia falls to the ground. Before he reaches the last picture, I rip it off the wall. With the end of the frame, I punch his nose. It knocks him back a step. The glass in the frame fractures like a spider web. Unfazed, he charges again, but before he takes another step, I jam the corner of the picture frame between his eyes. I hear a snap. His nose sinks into his face. The glass falls out of the frame. White bone pops out of red meat, where the frame hits him. Water forms in his eyes. With no glass to sturdy the frame, the square shape turns into a diamond. He comes at me again. I ram the picture frame deeper into his face until the frame breaks. A long, gilded piece of wood lodges in his face. He turns and falls to the ground. When he lands, the piece of wood pops out from the new hole in his face. His wrists curl like two snakes in fear, and his body erupts in a seizure. I lift the heel of my boot over his face and ram it down as hard as I can. This time, it's my boot heel instead of the picture frame driving into his head. Like a watermelon dropping to the ground, his head explodes. His limbs go limp.

I walk back and get Sophia off the ground, glass crunching under my blood-soaked boot. Then, I work my way to the living room. Where is everyone? All I've seen are dead bodies face down in the mud. Could everyone have been in the burning cabin? Locked in there by the Red Empire or maybe Roos. I start thinking the worst until I see Woody through the living room window, running with two Eaters giving chase.

I open the front door and step out to help Woody, but he's gone. He was running in the barn's direction. Maybe he already slipped inside. Maybe he was after his ax. Sophia is in a ready position. Each step is slow and cautious as I scan the grounds. There's still no sign of anyone else. I step inside the barn.

"Woody," I whisper.

My finger itches Sophia's trigger. Woody's ax rests in a stump. That would have been the first thing he picked up if he made it here. I peek into the stall where I sleep. Nothing. I turn to exit the barn, but before I do, I hear a man's voice whisper.

"Drift."

I walk toward the soft voice.

"Drift… down here."

Buried in the woodchips, I see Mac. I move away from the woodchips. He stands, and sawdust and pieces of wood fall off him.

"How did you get in there?" I ask him.

"Woody threw me down there and covered me with all those woodchips," he says.

"Did Woody come in here just now?" I ask.

"I didn't see him."

"Where's Jaysi, Mac?"

"Taken! The Ghost Villagers took her. They came in here with all these Eaters in chains. Everyone ran into the cabin, scared. It made it easy for the Ghost Villagers. With everyone gathered in one spot, they separated the males from the females. They put chains on the girls and marched them out of the village. They took Number One too. They let all the Eaters loose. The people in the burning cabin were fighting to get out, and the Eaters were fighting to get in. The screams, Drift! The screams were horrible."

I put my hand on Mac's shoulder.

"Woody was right to hide you, or you'd be dead too."

"I guess the negotiations didn't go good," Mac said.

"Not at all. They cut Number Two's head off."

I walk over to the rain barrel positioned under the barn roof. I cupped my hands and dip them in the water, washing the mud off my face and irrigating my eyes. I hear electricity and the smell of burning flesh. When I turn around, Mac is holding a long cylinder that has blue lighting sparking from the end. An Eater is lying facedown by me, shaking profusely. The Eater did his best to sneak up behind me. I pull Woody's ax from the stump. I swing it straight down on the Eater's head. The Eater stops shaking, but the ax gets stuck in its skull. I wiggle the ax handle. The Eater's head and neck jiggle back and forth until the ax dislodges from its head. Thick blood runs off the shiny metal. Looking at Mac and the rod he is holding, I ask him, "What the hell is that thing?"

Mac holds the rod outward and smiles.

"Well, I read they're called cattle rods or hotshots. They shock the hell out of you. I know that much."

It sounds like he is talking from experience. I take the ax and swing it back into the stump. Blood splatters from both sides of the ax.

Mac looks at the tip of the hotshot. He investigates the melted skin and small pieces of hair now attached to it. He pulls it close, and he almost vomits everywhere when he takes a whiff.

"Oh, man, that reeks!" he says.

"I will get Jaysi back," I tell him, not caring about his turning stomach.

"By yourself?"

"Who else is there, Mac?"

"You know I'm not a fighter, Drift, but if you need me, I'm going. I'll need a few things, but I'm going."

Mac rummages through his stuff. He pulls out a small metal drawer, and a few screwdrivers roll to the front. He pushes aside all the robotics on his desk. Little screws fall to the sawdust floor.

"Where's the revolver I gave you in the city, Mac? You lost it already!"

"I put it right here." Mac points to a metal drawer under his desk. "I can't find the bullets either." Mac stops looking and lifts his hotshot.

"Guess this will have to do," he says.

"Yeah, that'll light 'em up."

We walk out of the barn. The sun is high and bright, but the air is brisk and fresh. Woody appears from one of the muddy trails behind the barn, blood on his body, almost like a can of red spray paint exploded on him. He walks by me and Mac, never slowing down. He enters the barn and starts to wash his face and hands in the rainwater barrel.

"So, what's the plan?" he says.

"Kill 'em?" I say.

Mac points his hotshot rod in my direction. "And get the girls back. We have to."

The sun comes through the slats of the barn like stairs of light. Woody walks over to a burlap sack and picks it up. He starts to walk to Mac.

"I believe this is yours."

Mac grabs the sack and starts to unwrap it. It's his revolver and the bullets.

"I'm going too!" Woody says.

Neither Mac nor I tell him no.

"Let's move out," I say.

Woody walks back to his ax and pulls it out of the tree stump. When he throws it over his right shoulder, the ax head sticks out a few feet behind him.

We take the eastern trail and head out toward Ghost Village. Half a day into the hike, I'm exhausted. I realize I haven't slept or eaten in fourteen hours.

"The Red Empire's technology is so much more advanced. In five years, they are way ahead of the game," Mac says.

"It's easy when they're good at killing. They tell the best scientists and techies do it or die. And if they aren't scared of death, they kill the wives and kids. If they still refuse, they just kill them all and start again. With those terms, I'm sure a country can advance quickly."

"They left us to boil water and chop wood just to survive, and they—"

"I need to rest," I say. "I need my wits about me when we get to the village. I can't walk in delirious."

Mac and Woody agree to take a break from the path, so we wander off and settle near some large stones. As soon as my legs bend to sit, I feel the relief take over my body. I collapse onto the rock. The warmth of it against my back is comforting. Mac continues to talk. I can't tell if he is speaking to Woody or me. I can no longer keep up with the conversation, but his voice is soothing. It puts me right to sleep.

I wake up to Mac still talking. I glance around to get my bearings. I smell cooked meat. Woody is eating around the ribcage of a rabbit. He throws the back legs at me. They land on my lap. I pick them up and start chowing down. My energy is gone. I need to recharge. It's still daylight, which is good. We can hike more before we lose the day. Woody puts the fire out. He needed it long enough to cook the rabbit.

"Ready?" Woody asks.

"I am," I say. When I stand, my bones ache. I remember the Clif Bar Kyle gave me before the negotiations. The paper rips easily. The smell is delicious.

"What's that you got there?" Mac asks.

"A chocolate-chip bar."

I break it into three pieces and hand them out. Woody inhales his, not even pausing to chew. Mac smells it, then runs his tongue across it. He bites half of his third after his tongue approves of the flavor.

"Not bad," he says before throwing the rest in his mouth. We work our way back to the trail and hike again.

We're on the trail for thirty minutes when Woody says, "What the hell is that?" He points to feet sticking out from behind the green leaves of a rhododendron bush. The ankles are small.

"It could be a trap," I whisper.

I point to Mac to circle back down the trail and come from the backside. I motion to Woody to go up and around. I station myself on a slight slope on the opposite side of the trail and ready Sophia just in case. During the war, I remember a sniper who lured half a unit to their deaths in a similar scenario. He shot the first kid in his right kneecap. The kid fell to the ground, screaming in agony. Soldiers rallied to help him. The first rescue attempt failed. His buddy ran to save him, but he only made it halfway out before a bullet hit him right between the eyes. There was a second and third attempt. They all ended in the same result. Death. The sniper used the first kid as bait. Eventually, the unit wised up and stopped sending people. The kid crawled to safety the best he could. He almost made it until the sniper put a bullet right between his shoulder blades. The kid just dropped to his face. I saw the last bit of air come from his mouth. It's one of those memories that won't leave me.

The sniper's name was Gang, but we called him the Grey Wolf. The most famous sharpshooter of the war. No one knew his face. That's how tight-lipped the Red Empire was about him. I was sent on over thirty missions, hunting the Grey Wolf. Unsuccessful every time. We became rivals. After a while, I was more at war with him than with the Red Empire. If he killed one of ours, I'd kill two of theirs.

Reaching the body, Mac waves me over. I shake my head. I want to give it a few more minutes. "It's a girl. One of our girls."

Despite my better judgment, I jump from my position and hurry to the body, still looking up into the trees and out in the distance. It could still be a trap, but I can't stop myself. I have to know. I round the bush and spot a bloodstained rock. It's lying next to her head. Fear grips my spine, freezing me in place. The girl is face down, her hair a rat's nest, tangled and sticky with dried blood. I force myself to kneel next to the body. To gently flip her over.

It's not Jaysi.

My muscles loosen, and the intensity in my body relaxes. I am relieved it wasn't Jaysi but sad that I know who it was. It's the girl who was almost kidnapped a few days back. The ground around her body isn't disturbed, and all her clothes are still on.

"Why would they kill her?" Mac wonders.

"Why would anyone do anything like this to anyone?" Woody responds.

I noticed a small bloodstain on her arm, right below the wrist. It doesn't look like a splatter from her head. More like a tooth scratched her. If that's what I think it is, then she's bitten. When that bitten area rots, Eaters will swarm this place.

"Come on. We need to keep moving."

We make our way back to the trail. We keep heading east. The sun fades, and darkness overcomes the woods. The cold air surrounds us like a blanket of fear. It would have stayed daylight an hour longer if the thick branches of the hemlocks allowed it. We continue hiking through the night. Hours pass, and the smell of rotting flesh suddenly passes through my nose.

In the distance, I can see Ghost Village. Each entrance of the village has two fires blazing, making the shadows dance on the ground. The north and south entrance fires burn high as floating embers dance to the stars.

At the south gate, one of the ghost villagers stares into the fire. He takes a stick and pops it in and out of the flames, watching each time as the tip ignites. It burns for a second. Then his cheeks fill with air, and he gives it a big puff, extinguishing the flame. Like a wand, he twirls it around so fast that a streak of light chases after its glowing ember.

I walk up behind him with ease. His throat is no match for the blade of my knife. Grabbing his shoulders, I slide him to the outskirts of the firelight. Woody and I take his jacket off and throw it to Mac. Looking back down at the dead body, I see the markings on his hand. It's the same one the two kids that killed Stick had, only his is scarred over, not fresh.

With quickness, Mac puts the jacket on and sits on the bench. He rubs white mud on his face and applies streaks in his hair. He picks up the stick and leans forward to light the tip on fire, mimicking everything the kid was doing, except this time, he is keeping watch for us.

Woody goes left, and I go right, staying hidden behind the shacks. The pungent stench of rot and feces seeps through the cracks of each shack. It reeks of those Loco Solo villages I avoid at all costs. Inside the crevasses lurk shadows. I have no interest in looking through them. I am too focused on the two cages I saw through my scope at the negotiations if one could call them that. If the girls are here, that's where they will be.

Reaching the first cage, I take a knee in the mud. In front of me, red rusted metal wheels stick out of the mud. It looks like the cage is sinking in quicksand even though it rests solidly on the ground. How the hell did they get this massive thing over here, I wonder.

After more investigation, I notice half the shacks are old train cars. The wheels are so ancient. They're even older than the non-contact, electric-powered Maglev trains that used to bullet at three hundred miles an hour across the states. I look through the bars for familiar faces. The cages are crammed full of girls. Every face is dirty. All I see are the whites of their eyes looking at me. I lift my index finger when they get restless and tell them to keep quiet. After scanning the first cage, I reach the second one. I see Number One and Kyle balled up on the ground, trying to stay warm. There are both males and females in this cage, but fewer bodies.

"Pssst," I say.

They look up at me. Number One shakes his head, telling me no. I look around for danger, but I see nothing. Why is he shaking his head no? Ignoring his request, I step around the cage, kneeling to their eye level.

"Where's Jaysi?"

"She's in the other cage," Kyle whispers as he pokes his head over Number One's shoulder.

As he answers me, the cart behind me shakes like a small earthquake. Heavy breathing and pacing noises come from inside.

I turn to Number One. "What is that?"

Before Number One can answer, a thud comes from behind the wood. Something claws at the timber. A giant red eyeball looks through a knothole. For a split second, I make eye contact with it.

The creature breathes heavy. With each exhale, smoke swirls out through the seams of the boards. Slobber seeps through the cracks of the wood.

"A Beast!" I say to myself.

Number One taps my shoulder through the bars.

"Get out of here!" he says.

"The key? Where's the key?" I ask.

Kyle points to the crumbling building. This was where the shots were fired at me after the failed negotiations. It's where Roos retrieved the machete that sliced through Number Two's throat. My gut is churning in apprehension as I find myself in unfamiliar territory.

Whatever is in the car behind me continues to rake its claws against the wood, over and over. I can't help but think of how quickly it could take a life with those sharp claws. Then an earth-shattering roar erupts from inside. It starts as a deep, growling, beastly sound and builds until it's as loud as thunder. The noise is deafening. The people in the cages scramble back until they are pressed against the metal bars.

"Go… go!" Number One says under his breath.

I sneak into the dark shadow of the car, away from any light.

"All right, all right!" a voice in the distance yells.

Keeping to the darkness, I creep up on the building. Then I hear a reverberating sharp metal clanging. Turning around, I see Roos hitting the lock with his machete repeatedly. Snorting sounds come out of the vehicle in response.

"Shut up in there! You'll have dinner soon enough."

I have to get this key and get everyone out of that cage. I continue around to the back of the building. When I do, I notice the Red Empire HUV that had backed up to the library door earlier. This HUV must be how they got ahead of me when they chased me.

I get to the back door of the building. The door is missing. I walk up the three steps to the porch. The river rocks that make up the steps are uneven and loose. I make it onto the wrap-around porch and notice the door isn't missing. It's just shredded. Splinters lie everywhere. It looks like something ran out of it at full speed. I step inside the building, and it's warm even with the missing door. My nose starts to run with the temperature change. I turn my head to my shoulder and run my upper lip and the bottom of my nose across my shoulder, smearing snot across my sleeve.

I stay out of sight, though the lack of walls makes it difficult. Heavy velvet curtains have been nailed on top of the door frames. There is so much excess curtain it's bundled on the floor, kicked to the side so people can walk by it without tripping. I slide one curtain aside and carefully make my way around. I spot a yellow firelight glowing through a doorway and head for it.

When I arrive, I see that the curtain has been pulled back and held securely with a thin piece of rope tacked into the wall. I slip behind it and start scanning the large open room for the key. Roos enters through the front door.

"What's the ruckus about?" The voice comes from nowhere. I can't see the man who is speaking.

Roos laughs. "It's hungry."

"You mean she? She's hungry," the voice responds.

"Yeah! Whatever. It's so damn ugly I just rather call it, it."

"You know females are easier to control. The males are too territorial."

"Seems like a waste to me. Killing all these girls with that serum," Roos says.

I listen the best I can, catching fragments of their conversation. Roos sits down in a chair facing the direction of the voice.

"I want her," Roos says.

"You want a Beast?" the voice says, confused.

"No! The girl that smells like jasmine. I want her for myself. I don't want you to turn her," Roos says.

"Yessss, she is pretty."

I know they are talking about Jaysi, which causes my blood to boil. I lift my arm and wipe my nose on my shoulder again.

"Roos. The Red Empire has given me the honor of testing this serum and training these Beasts. She would make a fantastic Beast."

The door flies open, and two Ghost Villagers bring in a boy from Hill Top Village. I recognize him. He is the kid who fetches the water for the cook, Isabella.

"Ahhhh, yes. Welcome. Welcome," the voice says.

Roos walks over to the blazing fire and pulls out a long piece of iron, the end glowing red. The two Ghost Villagers hold the boy down and force his hand on the table. Roos walks over to the kid.

"This is going to hurt… a lot."

He shoves the searing-hot iron deep into the boy's palm, producing a loud, high-pitched scream from him. Smoke begins to curl off his sizzling skin. The pain must be unbearable.

As Roos removed the branding iron, a chunk of the boy's skin stays glued to the end. His cries cease. He holds his arm tightly, then watches as Roos puts the iron back in the fire.

"He turned quick. He wasn't even here an hour, and he wants to join us," Roos says.

Roos puts his hand on the back of the branded boy's neck.

"Stand up, brother," Roos says. "Welcome to the pack."

The two Ghost Villagers lead the boy to the door. The smell of burnt skin permeates the room now. I notice the box of ammo that was back at Hill Top Village. My ammo. It's here now. A jangling sound emits from Roos, and I notice a set of keys attached to his belt. Those must be the keys to the cage.

As Roos strides back and forth, I catch a glimpse of a red blanket trimmed in gold draped across a lap. It looks similar to the velvet curtains that hang from the doorway. The man slowly removes the blanket, revealing a long, steady object. My eyes widen as I recognize it. The same weapon I use—a sniper rifle.

"Grey Wolf," Roos says.

My stomach turns. It was the name I heard daily during the war, chilled into our bones like an icy winter wind. My unit used it as a metaphor for death, whispering, "Watch out for the Grey Wolf." He lived in the shadows, and we lived in fear.

My mind is swarming with my friends' faces, the ones he shot in my unit. There are too many souls for my brain to visualize. I shake my head to clear my thoughts. *Stop,* I say to myself. I will get myself killed if I don't stop with these thoughts. Taking in a few deep breaths, my blood starts to simmer.

"What about the shooter? He wasn't with the rest of the Hill Top peeps," Roos says.

"He'll find us. He always does. He could be behind me right now. I hunted for him the entire war. He's the best of the best. He'll find us."

I tuck back behind the curtain folds and surround myself with its darkness. The quick shift in movement makes the floor creak. I can't see the Grey Wolf or Roos, but they heard it. They had to. The quiet of the room is more deafening than a gunshot. *Run or move out the back?* I say to myself but stay where I am. I'll stand here until the morning if I have to.

Without warning, the curtain suddenly flies open. Roos rushes at me with blazing eyes and a raised machete. I barely have time to react as he swings the blade toward me, but I dodge it by an inch. He swings again. This time I grab the heavy curtains and use them as a shield against the sharp blade. The thick fabric is too much for the machete to cut through. Without hesitation, my legs start to move, and I sprint away.

"Release the Beasts!" the Grey Wolf screams out.

16

The moonglow gives the woods an uncanny feel. As I rush through the oak forest, it creates shadows of creatures and ghosts even though I know nothing is there. Not knowing what the Beasts look like has me on edge. I find myself out of breath and asking questions. What about Woody and Mac? And all the others? You can't just leave them back there. The trees become thicker and more familiar. Feeling safer, I take a moment. I keep looking in all directions. My chest expands and contracts as I breathe in the cold air. With every exhale, clouds of vapor exit my mouth. The cold air burns my lungs as I struggle to get a full breath. The gentle light of the moon reveals my ragged breathing. Wisps of smoke curl from my lips with each exhale.

After scouting the area, I feel I have enough distance between the Beast and me. A low-hanging limb catches my eye. I struggle to hold Sophia and pull myself up. I get some sure footing and climb onto the limb. It's quiet. That's what worries me. I hear nothing. Not even the screams from Ghost Village. I couldn't have run that fast that far.

I maneuver into a more comfortable position on the limb. The limb is big enough for me to lie flat on my stomach. I put the butt of my rifle under my arm and aim down the path. Soon as I'm situated, I hear snorting. It's not the wild boar kind of snort. Not a horse. No, this is new to me.

The low forceful exhaling has a primal, authoritative sound as it gets closer and louder. At first, all I can see is the shapes of trees and their shadows, until a pair of red dots emerge from the dark. They are the same size, and they are symmetrical. A pair of eyes. When the moon hits them just right, they reflect like dog eyes but are more prominent. They are as red as the T8's red target I aim for. For a second, they give the Beast's position away. Then they disappear.

Moments later a thick, humid mist covers my face. I can hear soft breathing in the air. This isn't fog at all. My hand moves away from the gun and inches toward my knife. Keeping my balance is challenging as all my weight is on my chest while I search. The Beast is right behind me. If I make any sudden movements, I'm dead. The stench around me grows stronger. Its breath smells of Eaters and rotting flesh. She's behind me now. I have to make a quick, blind decision. Without a second thought, I turn and roll off the limb. Looking up at the Beast, my body falls through the air as I fight to free my knife from its sheath. The Beast roars and lunges forward in rage. The ground comes quick. I land flat on my back. The wind gets knocked out of my lungs like it's escaping without me. I watch as the Beast falls toward me. I roll to one side. My shortness of breath momentarily paralyzes me. The Beast lands right on top of me, knocking me flat again. Its left paw, or rather a claw, lands on my scope. The glass shatters.

I get a good view of the Beast's face for the first time. Its eyes are more snakelike than doglike. Its diamond-shaped pupils glow red. Its hair is that of a hard and coarse porcupine or a giant hog, but I feel if I touched it, it would slice my skin like a razor. It has a long snout with a bat-shaped nose dripping with mucus. The ears are short and hairless, like devil horns that are flat black with pinkish veins racing through them. Its teeth are long and sharp. The slobber and drool run off from its teeth like a waterfall, soaking my shirt. I can see its bloodstained teeth clear as day.

I grip the buck knife as tightly as I can and thrust the blade up and through its lower jaw with all my power. The knife goes in and out of the top of its snout. With my palm on the bottom of the knife, I give it a little extra thrust. I keep pushing the blade up. The Beast throws its head back, rising to her hind legs. I have enough time to roll out from underneath it before her two claws come back down.

It can't roar. The blade has sealed the snout to the bottom jaw. It can only snort and give little growls deep inside her throat. It swings its claw at me, knocking me back a few feet. It starts pawing at the knife. Blood trickles out of the creature's nostrils as I scramble up from the ground. The Beast rocks back and forth vigorously, trying to dislodge the weapon stuck in its snout. Each time it stands up on its hind legs and jerks its skull around, the knife inches out a bit further. The creature is over ten feet tall when it is upright.

The Beast thrashes its head from side to side, unlocking the blade from its snout. With a mighty snort, it sprays blood and snot all over me. I react like lightning, diving forward and grabbing the knife off the ground. A steady flow of blood drains from its snout as it rears back and hits me, causing me to fly ten feet through the air.

With no hesitation, I jump to my feet. The Beast drops back to all fours. Free from the knife, it lets out a roar. I run full speed with the blade pointed at its head. Before it can react, the blade goes through its right eye, sinking five inches past its eyelid. Its right claw starts to convulse. It doesn't roar. It doesn't growl. It exhales one last breath and collapses. It's dead. I pull my knife from its eye socket, wiping away the red-purple blood from the blade. I try to use its coarse fur, but it smears the blood. I feel like collapsing, but I need to get back to Jaysi. In my brief rest, I hear the power of rushing water near me until a wretched roar pierces the night air. It's another Beast. I'm so weak I can't face another one. Desperate, I head toward the river, hoping the Beast will lose my scent if I cross it. I come out where the tree line meets the rocks of the river. From where I am, it has to be forty yards across. The current is swift. The river is so loud it almost drowns out the sounds of the night. Let's just hope it doesn't drown me.

The moonlight bounces off the ice-covered rocks and makes the moss sparkle. I cautiously walk on the icy rocks, heading to the river's edge. When I sink my boot in the water, it feels like hundreds of sharp needles pricking me at once. My body temperature drops. The coldness is unbearable; my teeth chatter uncontrollably, and the stones beneath me shift with each step. Struggling to find something to hold onto, I slip and tumble into the river, where the rapids carry me a few feet down. Using my outstretched arms, I eventually grab onto a large rock that sticks out of the rapids. My hands and fingers are numb from the cold water, but I find solid ground to stand on. The water swirls around my legs, and the current tries to drag me under again. The tops of the light gray rock darken when my water-soaked body brushes against it. Each step is slow and tedious as I wade to the other side. I step out of the water when I reach the river's edge. I have twenty feet of rocks and boulders to the tree line. It's hard keeping my balance. Each step is slow and painful. I can no longer feel my feet or toes, so it is near impossible to stand, much less walk. I stop and collapse behind a fallen tree. Catching my breath, I start to breathe into the palms of my hands, trying to put feeling back into my fingers. Staying behind the fallen tree, I peek through its twisted root system. I see the Beast sniffing the air. My whole-body cries in pain. I remain still. I start to breathe out of my nose so vapor from my mouth doesn't give me away. I have one eye peeking through the roots at her, but she spots me. She snorts, and smoke shoots from her nostrils and curls around her snout. She starts clawing the ground. She seems pissed.

Turning and positioning myself, I rest Sophia on the tree trunk. My right eye looks through the scope, but the glass is broken. It's useless. The Beast rushes into the rapids. It trudges through the water at first, slipping on the same algae rocks I did. Sophia was submerged under that cold water just like I was. Her barrel is cold. If a bullet flies through the barrel, it could crack her. The temperature change will be extreme. I know the military-issued bullets are lacquer-sealed, but what if the seal doesn't hold? Sophia might not fire at all. If water seeps into the bullets, I'm done. So many things can go wrong right now, but I have to try. Hoping to get lucky, I pull the trigger on Sophia. *Peeuwoooooo.* Water sprays up to the left of the Beast. My fingers are numb. I can't feel the trigger. With the palm of my hand, I lift the bolt and reload a new bullet. I know the motion but can't feel what I'm doing. I just trust my instinct.

The Beast is halfway across the rapids now. The reload took too long. I take aim through the useless scope again. *Peeuwoooooo.* The bullet had to hit her, but it didn't slow her down. I start scratching my finger on the cold metal. I can feel the pressure of the trigger on my index finger. I just can't feel the trigger. Come on, come on, I tell myself. Trying to get the feeling back in my fingertip, I catch myself breathing out of sync. The cold has my heart working overtime. I try breathing normally to calm my nerves. As I take a deep breath, I notice the Beast getting its footing now. Its head turns into a head and neck, and then the head and neck turn into a head, a neck, and shoulders. It has its footing now. It rises out of the rapids. I stop halfway through exhaling. As soon as the Beast emerges from the cold water, it lets out an ear-piercing roar. That little second it took to bellow out a roar is all I need. *Peeuwoooooo.* Direct hit. The bullet goes right through her left eye. The Beast collapses and falls on the river rock, its hind legs still in the water.

Freezing and shaking, I eject my magazine and reload it. I want a complete run of bullets in case there's another Beast. Twenty minutes go by. I know the sun is rising. A beautiful, yellow-tinted sky emerges behind the mountaintop. I'm hopeful the warmth will be coming soon. With weak legs, I stand, forcing myself to get my circulation going. Walking over to the dead Beast, my boots drag over the rocks. Ice has formed over my clothes, and I can't stop shivering.

The Beast's body is now visible, its fur mangy and filthy. The muscles bulge behind its coarse bristle hair. A streak of white runs down its neck like a lightning bolt, prominent against the otherwise dark hair. I unsheathe my knife and plunge it into the Beast's stomach. Its insides spill out, and an unbearable smell fills the air. I grab all the guts and throw them out into the rushing rapids. They float away as quickly as I can throw them in. I climb inside the still-warm carcass and curl up.

I'm not sure how long it takes, but the feeling in my limbs returns. I separate the skin to get a view outside and let in some fresh air. When I do, I hear splashing water. I close the skin back. The carcass shakes. Then nothing. The splashing suddenly stops. Time crawls with the silence. Maybe it's safe to look now. I reach to separate the skin, but before I do, I feel a heavy weight fall on my chest, like two hands pushing inward. The carcass rocks back and forth. Muffled grunts come from outside. I hear sniffing sounds from where I cut the Beast open. I take tiny breaths so the Beast's stomach doesn't inflate or deflate. A lower, soft roar makes it apparent it's another Beast. Sniff after sniff, the Beast walks in a circle around me, grunting and snorting. Every so often, it shakes the carcass like it's trying to wake its friend. The sniffs grow distant. I lift a small piece of the cut skin to see the large Beast walking to the fallen tree I hid behind earlier. The Beast pauses, lifting its head up high to sniff the air. It starts to make its way back to me. It knows my scent now. Being inside this dead carcass is throwing it off. I fold the skin in so I can get a better grip. If it shakes me again, I don't want to pop out. My fingers pinch the top and bottom slits together. I'm holding it tight. My fingers start going numb. This time from lack of circulation, not the cold.

Splash!

The Beast jumps back into the rapids. It has got to be crossing the rapids now. I stay inside the carcass for another twenty minutes, just in case.

Eventually, I climb out of the Beast and think to myself, if I had been passing by and saw this Beast's stomach moving, and then a human popped out of it, it would have freaked me out. My body is sore but warm as I stand up. Steam rises from my body. I squat down and splash my face. The water is cold but refreshing. What appears to be fat, veins, and guts fall from my head and face. The stomach juice makes my shirt start to harden.

Once my hands and face are clean, I unscrew my scope. It frees itself from the top of my rifle, and I drop it to the ground. I have no use for it, and it's beyond repair. No need to carry dead weight. Instead of walking back across the rapids and freezing again, I walk down the river.

After an hour of walking, I see a bridge in the distance. It is greenish in color. It lives in the mountain's shadow year-round, so moss and algae grow on it. The water below it flows through cut stone arches. At this vantage point, the masonry is stunning. Knowing it's hundreds of years old and still standing adds to the coolness. I head toward the bridge, excited I don't have to wade through the water this time. I hear voices from the bridge's top side when I get closer. The water is moving too fast to hear their conversation, but I'm thankful to know they are there. Sneaking a little deeper away from the river, I get a better view. A Red Empire patrol vehicle is blocking the bridge. Two Ghost Villagers are talking to a patrolman who is sitting on the hood of the black HUV. Four total humans. When I finish with these guys, I'm going to steal their patrol craft. That will get me back to the Ghost Village a whole lot quicker than walking. Dropping to a sitting position, I lift my left knee. My clothes smell of raw sewage and rotten fish. Lucky for me, the wind isn't blowing right now. I rest Sophia on my knee, my left hand under the butt. This way, I can hold her steadier, and she won't slip from my shoulder. With no scope, the extra steadiness will be helpful. Now that I'm without a scope, I'll need to adjust my aperture sights. Taking a deep breath, I ready myself. I know I have to be faster than normal because they are standing near a six-barrel, M134-type mini-gun. That thing can spit out six thousand rounds a minute, so I don't want to give any of them a chance to get behind that thing and light me up. I exhale halfway. I start to pull the trigger back slowly and firmly. My finger can feel the metal this time.

I feel the weight of the trigger about to release. Something hits me below my right arm. Right in my rib cage. *Peeuwoooooo.* My bullet strikes the hood of the HUV. I slide across the ground for ten to fifteen feet, dropping my rifle. I put out my hands to keep myself from slipping, but it does no good. My back hits a tree, stopping me. I let out a grunt. When I get to my knees, I see the large Beast. I look for my rifle. It's too far away at this point to do me any good. I reach down to my belt to pull out my buck knife. When I do, I notice her nails are about the same length as my blade.

Getting to my feet, I try to get a full breath. The pain from my rib cage causes me to flinch. The men from the bridge start to scream, alerting each other where I am.

I hear the buzz of 6,000RPM electric barrels start spinning on the HUV. When the barrel hits the needed speed to shoot, bullets start rushing into the woods. I can see the vegetation falling to the left of the Beast. Daylight shines brighter through the canopy of the trees as limbs fall. My first instinct is to dart off to the right, but this Beast is faster than I am. I take a few steps back and find my back against the tree that had stopped me.

The Beast lunges at me. I fall to the ground, flat on my back. I have one defense. I lift my legs. As the Beast falls, it lands on my feet. It weighs a ton. My knees start to buckle and come down to my chest. The Beast swings its left claw at me. I lift the Beast with all the power left in my legs. My thighs begin to shake and burn. I hear the bullets sink deep into its back. Thump, thump, thump, thump. Its body looks as if it's having a seizure. Every time a new lead goes inside it, it shakes. The Beast roars in pain. My legs give out, and it falls on top of me. I struggle with the weight. I'm not able to get out from under it. Which is a good thing at first since they keep sending bullets this way. I inch my way from under it. I hold it between the bullets and me. The tree behind me splinters from the bullets that sweep the forest.

I need my rifle, but Sophia is in the ferns. Debris is everywhere. The forest floor holds the remains of all the tattered shrubbery and vegetation.

Then the bullets stop. A second later, the buzz from the spinning barrel stops as well. He's out of bullets. Now's my chance. I crawl over to find Sophia. Grabbing her, I continue to crawl into the woods. I hear one of the patrolmen yelling.

"West! He's west of us!"

I can hear the screaming jets of a drone. My legs are shaking. With no backpack—just my rifle and a few extra bullets—I climb a tree as fast as I can. When I reach the top, my visibility increases ten-fold. I can see the patrol HUV from up here.

"Switch to infrared then!" a patrolman screams into a walkie.

Who's he talking to? Who's on the other end of that walkie?

Then, a Striker Drone comes in out of nowhere, dropping straight down from the sky. The engines scream as it stops in front of the Beast, dust from the ground swirling around them. It hovers there, doing a 360-visual. The coarse hair of the Beast moves while the drone's thrusters continue to blow down on it. It's loaded down with ammo. I know because of how much power it takes to hover. The heat sensor is on the bottom of the drone, so it hasn't detected me yet. It starts to spin in a circular motion as it rises higher in the air. I stand a chance in these woods if I can just send a bullet through the infrared sensor. It reaches eye level with me. It circles and faces me. I know it detects me when it stops spinning. A small red light is flashing on the belly of the drone. *Peeuwoooooo.* I pull the trigger. The bullet hits the target. The drone starts to spin out of control. *Peeuwoooooo.*

I send another round, hoping to hit something vital on it. I hit the fuel tank. It doesn't explode, but it's leaking fuel. Now the Striker Drone is spinning and rising into the sky, higher and higher. I've never seen one do this before. I must have hit controls or communications. When it reaches the clouds, it runs out of fuel. The Striker Drone falls, flipping end over end and spinning. Like me, the Red Empire patrol and the Ghost Villagers watch it fall back to earth. When they realize it's about to fall on them, it's too late. It crashes on top of the HUV craft and explodes on impact. The force of the explosion pushes me backward. I reach out, grasping for a limb to catch myself. All I grab is air. Sophia's strap falls from my shoulder to my forearm. I reach for a branch as gravity starts taking me to the ground. As I do, Sophia swings and hits my rib cage, where the Beast hit me. The pain is sharp and sudden, but I manage to grip a branch. I secure my footing and start to climb down the tree. A smoke cloud rises into the sky like a mushroom. I'm sure there was more than extra ammo on that Striker Drone. Time to get out of here.

Avoiding the heat from the flames as best I can, I start to cross the bridge. The heat is intense. It's crazy. I was freezing inside some animal's stomach an hour ago, trying to stay warm. Now, I'm sweating. Two bodies are burning. Two must have escaped the explosion. I'm not sure if the ones burning are patrolmen or Ghost Villagers. Once I reach the bridge's other side, I walk down to the river. I get down on my knees and cup my hands, sinking them under the water, lifting them to my mouth, and drinking. The cold water is refreshing after that kind of heat and smoke.

18

Mac is walking down the trail. He looks exhausted. He can barely lift his legs high enough to put one foot in front of the other. With each step, his boots scuff the ground. I want to yell at him, but I can't. I stay ten feet off the trail, hidden. He wobbles over to a rock a few yards off the trail. I sneak over to him. I don't want him to scream, so I whisper his name.

"Mac." He looks in all directions. I step out from behind the tree.

"Drift! You're alive…"

He attempts to get up, but his bottom falls back onto the rock.

"Sorry, Drift. My legs have had it."

I kneel down so I'm at eye level with him. My heart is racing. I'm seeing someone I thought I would never see again. Mac never makes eye contact with me. I can tell he is in shock.

"I saw you run into the woods. Then those huge dog—were-wolf things, or…whatever they are, took off running after you. I thought they got you. They had your scent. Oh man, speaking of scent. Why do you stink so bad?"

"Well, they didn't get me. I'm here." I put both my hands on Mac's face. He smiles back at me. A moment later, his nose twitches. He leans forward and takes a few more whiffs. Shaking his head, he squints his eyes at how bad I smell.

"Oh, man. You reek! That's not from going without a shower. That smells like you rolled around in something rotten!"

I laugh, then quickly sober. "Where's Woody?" I asked.

"I left him. The Ghost Villagers went nuts, crowing like birds. That Roos kid let those animals loose. When they started chasing you, Jaysi screamed. Roos was pissed. Like real pissed. I think he was jealous that Jaysi was worried about you. He opened the cage and took her inside the cabin."

"What happened to Jaysi, Mac?"

Mac struggles but stands.

"As far as I know, she's fine, Drift. She's in that cabin."

Mac sits back down. I sit on the ground and lean my back on the rock he is sitting on. We need our strength, so we rest. Mac hands me some venison jerky he packed before our trip and an almost empty water bottle, so I drink the rest. My stomach is still empty but swelling from the water hitting the jerky in my belly. That should hold me over for a while.

"You're going back, aren't you?" he asks.

"Yes. Yes, I am, Mac. You don't have to go! It'd be great if you did, but you don't have to go."

"No way," Mac says short and blunt. "I'm going with you!" I hand the water bottle back to him. It's empty, but he likes saving those things to reuse them. He puts it back in his backpack. Somewhere in there, I fall asleep. When I wake up, I sit up too quickly. For some reason, I forgot I was in the woods. I'm disoriented. The rapid movement jolts a sharp pain from my rib cage. It's a swift reminder of where I am. I can breathe, but it's not as easy. Somewhat rested but still sore, Mac and I make our way back to Ghost Village.

When we arrive on the outskirts of the village, I do some reconnaissance. No one is walking the perimeter of the village. It's odd.

As we emerge from the tree line, we hustle across a few feet of mud to the train car. We are even more conservative in the daylight with our movements and hiding spots. We put our backs against the warm wood. The good part about the sunlight is I can see the train tracks. They head north out of the village. I guess that's why they had two guards on it last night. There are no canopies of trees above the tracks. Looking down the track lines, they disappear at the bend.

I come out from behind the train car we were leaning on. Number One and Kyle are sitting cross-legged in the cage. Kyle unwraps his legs and crawls to the bars. His hands sink deep in the mud.

"Drift! Get me out of here!" Kyle says.

"Is Jaysi in the other cage still?" I ask.

"No…some old man with gray hair took her. Said he was taking her into town and using her as bait. He's setting you up, Drift. He's going to kill you."

I start to notice the emptiness of the village. No one is crowing. No one is chasing me. I begin to make my way to Grey Wolf's hut. Mac grabs my arm to stop me.

"Where are you going?" he asks.

"I'm going to see if the keys are in that cabin."

I work my way up the front steps. As quiet as the village is, I start hearing a jingling sound. It gets louder and louder. The front door swings open. The force of the door causes the wind to blow my hair back. It hits the wall and falls off its rusted hinges. Roos charges out of the building. He continues toward me, fearless and strong-willed. He tightens his grip on his machete, turns his hips, and swings with enormous strength at my head. My right foot finds the edge of the step. Even though I just walked up to them, I forgot the steps were there.

I fall back. He misses my head by inches. As I fall back, Sophia slips off my shoulder. She lands in the mud to my right. Roos saunters down the steps. I don't have time to grab Sophia. I hurry to my feet. The mud falls off my back. He comes down the steps and starts lifting the machete over his head with both hands, exposing his stomach. I clench my hand as tightly as possible and swing at his rib cage. A solid hit. His machete starts to come down, and I charge at him. He slips on the steps and falls backward. His spine runs the edge of each step. He grunts from the impact. I feel him tense up. In this split second, I take advantage by punching his temple. Roos accelerates his knee up between my legs, making contact. The pain shoots into my stomach and returns me to the muddy ground. I land in arms' reach of Sophia. Roos gets up quicker than I do. I try to point Sophia in Roos's direction and pull the trigger, but he kicks her out of my hand. As I watch Sophia soar through the air and land in the mud, he gets another kick into my rib cage. Falling to my back, I grab my ribs. He raises his face to the sky and crows a loud, keening sound. I get to my knees before he can make any sudden moves.

A few Ghost Villagers emerge from the train cars when they hear Roos crowing. They appear to be the youngest of the villagers. They gather around us and, in unison, start crowing.

"What do we have here?" Roos says. He paces. "Hmm, this seems familiar to me. Where's your little white flag, Shooter Boy?"

"Where's Jaysi?" I ask.

"Jaysi? Oh, so that's her name. Hmm, pretty name. She wouldn't tell me what it was when I asked." Roos taps his dirty index finger to his lips, almost like he is having a genius moment.

"I'll be saying that name a lot tonight."

"I'll make you an offer, Roos," I say.

"An offer. What can you offer me, Shooter Boy?"

"You let us go, and I won't kill you."

Roos laughs.

"Kill Me! Oh, man. That's funny." His laughing stops, and he raises his voice to a shouting level. "You hear that, boys? I think we have a deal here. If he kills me, we let them all go."

The villagers stop crowing. Roos circles behind me and stops. I can feel the wet mud soaking into the material of my pants. I remember Number Two's knees sinking in the mud like mine. I get this overzealous feeling that I've been down here long enough. I hear the blade brush Roos's pant leg. I know his trick. I saw it with my own eyes. He's about to swing at my head. When he lifts his machete, his shadow on the ground gives him away. I hear the blade move through the air. I fall to the left and roll. The wind created by the swinging machete whizzes by my ear. It slices a few hairs as it passes. I get to my feet and take a fighting stance. I watch the look on Roos's face turn. His smile falls away to a weighted concern.

"Ok, military boy, let's have some fun," he says.

He acts like he will swing his machete again but swings a fist instead. His left hand flies into my cheekbone. Orbs of light dance behind my eyelids, but I keep my feet. I was expecting the machete. He caught me off guard. I'm sure it would have knocked me out if I didn't turn my head at the last minute. With all his weight on his left foot, I roll myself back under his arm as quickly as possible. My hand leaves the side of my hip and rams straight up into his ribs. I feel movement underneath the skin. That particular part of his body turns to jelly. I got him good. There's no time for celebration. When Roos draws back, he swings his machete slower than the times before. I dodge it. Or at least I thought I did. It slices the top of my shoulder, cutting through my jacket. It isn't deep, but it stings. No, it burns like fire. He doesn't reset his position, just rotates his wrist, so the machete blade is aimed back at me, and swings it. He knew the first blow caught me off guard. I step back, and it misses me this time. When I dodge it, the blade's momentum hits one of the crowing spectators. The machete sinks deep into the side of his skull. Roos struggles to pull it back out but can't. It's lodged in the bone too deep. I attack, knowing Roos is focused on getting the blade loose. I launch another punch to the same section I already bruised or broke. Roos clutches his side, dropping his elbow to guard his ribs. I hit his elbow, but by the look on his face, he felt the blow. I pretend to swing to the same spot. He tightens his arm to block it, but I throw my other fist instead. It isn't as hard of a punch as I wanted, but it lands right under his chin in his throat. He drops to his knees, choking and gasping for air. I must have collapsed his esophagus. I walk around him. His eyes are glazed over from lack of oxygen and coughing.

"This seems familiar," I say.

As I get behind him, I choke him in a headlock. I feel a burning sensation come to my forearm. My hold loosens. A small knife is sticking out when I let go and pull my arm back. At first, I can't believe it doesn't hurt, but the pain comes when I see the knife in my arm. I slide the knife out from my forearm. I hold it tight and swing as fast as I can. I cut him four times. The cuts are quick. Roos doesn't even see them. I slice the top of his hand. When he goes to inspect the cut, I run the blade across his right ear, splitting it in two. He reaches for his ear to cover it. A stream of blood runs down his neck. Instead of swinging the knife, this time, I bring it down like Woody swinging his ax. The blade enters his chest. He falls to his right side. The left side of his face sinks deep in the mud. I grab the handle to pull the knife out. When I do, I realize Roos isn't breathing. I let the knife go and lift my arms.

"I kept my word. Now keep yours."

Mac rushes over to Roos and unties the keys from his hip. The villagers are too young and too scared to react.

"Got 'em!" Mac says as he lifts the keys in the air. He rushes over and starts unlocking the cages. Somber and slow, people spill out into the sunlight. They walk over to me.

"They needed our girls to turn them into Beasts. They let them feed on the Eaters. That's their plan to rid the Eaters," Number One explains.

"Creating a problem to solve a problem," Mac says.

"Where did they take Jaysi?" I ask.

Number One points down the train tracks.

"That way. They hauled her off in that large cargo HUV."

Looking at Number One, I tell him, "Take them into the mountains. I'm going after Jaysi." It doesn't take long before Mac says, "I'm going too."

"Me too," Number One says.

"Has anyone seen Woody?" I ask.

No one has an answer. I start walking toward the tracks, and the Ghost Villagers return to their train cars. Through their windows, they watch us. With no one stepping up to help Roos, I wonder if they were forced to be here.

By the time we reach the track, the sun is setting. The Hill Top Villagers walk in the opposite direction than us. Kyle walks toward me. I figure he's just going to wish me luck.

"I'm not a good fighter, but I'll pull my weight."

19

As we walk down the tracks, we pass vacant industrial buildings, abandoned rock quarries, and tobacco barns. We put in half a night of walking before stopping to sleep. We rise with the sun and continue. The city comes fast, and the tracks dead end in an old train yard. Like an iron cobweb, the tracks splinter off in many different directions.

"Where are we going?" Number One asks.

"Should we go to the library?" Kyle says with half his usual confidence.

Sounds good to me, I think to myself. That's where Grey Wolf took the Beast to feed on the Eaters. I assumed the Red Empire was responsible for gathering Eaters for the Beasts, and Grey Wolf was responsible for turning the girls into the Beasts. That would be a good place to start.

The university is on the other side of town. We don't have time to walk around the city, so we go through it. Jaysi is running out of time. Is Grey Wolf turning her into a Beast to get to me? Is he keeping her as a trophy?

The empty train cars are eerie as we walk by them. With their magnets turned off, they just lie on the ground. Most of them are toppled over. Some were lucky enough to land flat.

I remember, as a kid, I got to ride one. I believe it was Christmas. We were going to see my grandma on the Coast. We could have driven, but I begged Dad to take the train. It hovered a foot off the ground, and the sound was soothing, like wind through hemlock trees. It traveled a hundred and fifty miles an hour. Well, the one we rode in did. We couldn't afford the express train. Honestly, I wouldn't have wanted it to get there any faster. The train ride was fantastic. It was a dream come true for a seven-year-old. It didn't even feel like we were moving. I remember starting at the back of the train car and running full speed to the front of it. I kept telling my dad I was faster than the train. The past keeps sneaking in and out of my thoughts.

We keep walking and walking. The sun is at its highest peak now. Dead noon. It's not above us. In the winter, it always sits lower in the sky than in the summer. We are here. We walk into the shadow of a massive condominium high-rise. I stop walking. *The Grey Wolf,* I say to myself. *What am I doing?* Being unfocused and daydreaming will get me killed. We are all out in the open. No more! Get back into survival mode. Get back to the mission! Save Jaysi.

"The Grey Wolf will be in a high position," I tell everyone as I point up to the condos.

Number One asks, in a confused voice, "Who?"

"The Grey Wolf!"

"You know him?" Number One asks.

"I know of him. Everyone in the war knew of him. He was famous, like the devil or the grim reaper. His name meant death."

Mac looks up at the condo. "Not the kind of famous person I want to meet."

If we stay out in the open, they will learn how he became so famous.

"He loves traps. He doesn't just shoot: he plays games," I told them.

We come to the corner of the high-rise. We scout up and down the street. It's empty. I look up in the high-rise to see if there are hiding spots for the Grey Wolf, a place I would set up in if I were him. The parking garage across the street will keep us hidden better than the shadow of this high-rise. I dart over to take refuge in the garage. The others hustle behind me. The floor, the walls, and the ceiling are all made of cold gray concrete. Once inside the garage, I scan the area. We weave in and out of the parked HUVs.

The shadows inside the garage are dark even for this time of day. If the Grey Wolf took a high position, we are in serious trouble. Especially with Eaters walking in the shadows.

The wind starts circulating through the garage like a wind tunnel, and the smell of rotting corpses rides in on the wind. Mac's eyes water, and Number One begins to cough. I put my hand on Number One's mouth and press hard. He looks up at me. I lift my index finger over my lips.

As quietly as possible, I whisper, "Shhh. We need to be as quiet as possible in places like this."

Number One and Kyle nod at me. Kyle stretches out the neck of his shirt and lifts it over his nose and mouth. Mac and Number One copy him. The smell is worse than walking around a Loco Solo village, but as bad as it smells, the garage keeps us hidden. We reached the other side of the garage, an entire block away.

Kyle reaches the other side first, looks over the railing, and sees the town. "No way!" he says under his breath. When we all get to the metal railing to look over, I notice the street runs downhill. We entered the garage at street level, but now it seems we're on the second or third floor.

"Look there." Kyle points to an electrical chain-link fence covering the whole city block across from us. The war left its mark on this town. There are craters from what looks like 1,000 lb. bombs everywhere inside the fence. It isn't the craters that shock us. It's what is going in them. Corpses. Mountains of motionless, stiff Eaters piled on Eaters. There are two unmanned excavating robots busy at work. They have the word "Exa-Bot" written in flat black on the side of their gray doors. One is carving a crater deeper. The other is pushing Eaters into the crater. Are they starving to death?

On the one hand, I'm happy to see they're all dead, but on the other, it means the Red Empire is one step closer to moving in. When the Eaters are all gone, so are we. It's like burying hope.

Outside the electric fence is a patrol HUV. Two soldiers stand guard at the entrance. One starts to dig in his front breast pocket. Walking to the gate, he pulls out a magnetic key that looks like a business card. He swipes his card over the magnetic pad. When he does, the red light on the pad turns green. The gate unlocks and starts to swing open. A dump HUV rounds the corner and enters through the gate. It's huge. It has to take gallons of fuel to stay in the air. It's more deafening than the patrol HUVs. Even louder than the Striker Drone that almost killed me the other day.

A man wearing a full-body HAZMAT suit waves to the driver, getting his attention. He points to the most crammed crater and gives him a few hand gestures, guiding him in. He cups both his hands, mimicking the act of dropping water out of his cupped hands. The dump HUV driver must know what it means because he hovers over the crater's center. A hatch from the bottom of the dump HUV opens, and stiff bodies pour out, falling onto the mountain of already dropped torsos and limbs. This time, the bodies are Eaters and non-Eaters. Now I know why they have a gate around the dead bodies. Eaters would get full bellies if they could get to those bodies, but the Red Empire wants them gone like they want us gone.

Mac and Number One back away from the railing. I can tell that the image affected them. It's burned into their brains now for the rest of their lives. I still remember my first charred body, my first headshot, and seeing the skin peeled off by the teeth of an Eater. This is just another first. The last thing I need is another first. I am in awe of how many bodies there are. I start studying the condo high-rise behind us.

Kyle taps my shoulder. "Drift...we don't need to go to the library anymore."

"Why?"

Kyle points down a street to a crosswalk bridge that connects two buildings. It's about eleven stories off the ground. The buildings appear to be an old hospital, about thirty stories high. There are so many windows that the reflecting sun is blinding. There is no roof over the walkway. It has handrails made of aluminum or titanium. Under the bridge, I see her. Dangling from a rope, I see Jaysi. Her hands are above her head and tied together. She dangles at least fifty feet from the bridge and above the street. A dozen Eaters circle below her. They can't reach her, but they know she is there. It's another game for the Grey Wolf. He has two buildings on either side of Jaysi, the sun blinding us from this side, and Eaters on the ground. There's one way to get Jaysi.

"We have to save her," Number One says in a soft low tone.

"She already looks dead just hanging there like that," Mac says.

I pray he's wrong. Either way, we're about to find out.

20

We walk to the garage stairwell. I give Kyle and Mac the job of infiltrating the hospital building on the left while Number One takes the right. All the while trying not to be eaten by the Eaters in the middle. I have to find a position to see Grey Wolf's muzzle flash or a scope reflection. If he takes the bait, the bait being Kyle, Mac, and Number One. It's not the best plan, but a plan.

Outside the garage, we split up. I peek around the corner to ensure there aren't any Eaters, Beasts, or Patrolmen.

"All clear," I say.

They all head in their designated directions. I stay where I am, looking back at the condos. The concussions from 1,000 lb. bombs have taken their toll on the glass. It has the perfect line of sight to see Jaysi. I'd lie on my stomach about five feet back in one of those units. No one would see my muzzle flash or my scope. That's where I would be.

I have a full magazine and a bullet in the chamber. My best position would be the hospital rooftop, but that's a dead giveaway. Besides, this time of day, the sun would blind me looking back at the condos. No. I have to find a position that no one will expect. Standing in the exit corridor, I notice the Exa-Bot shut down. It becomes super quiet. It parks itself in front of a mobile-charging station. The guy in the HAZMAT suit jumps in the last dump HUV and speeds out of the gate.

That's it. That's my spot. I make my way down the street, staying out of sight in the condo's shadows. There is an alley that spills out in front of the gate where the guards are standing. The Eaters are focused on Jaysi right now, and the guards are focused on their phones more than the gate.

I have two options. Kill the guards and grab the keys, but the gunshot will give me away. Or jump on top of their HUV and over the fence. If I do the latter, I better have an exit strategy, or I'll be stuck behind that electrical buzzing fence all night. The Exa-Bot is parked close to the fence. I could climb onto the charging station, onto the Exa-Bot, and then jump over the fence. That's the plan. That's my escape route. Sounds easy enough.

I have to distract the guard somehow. More Eaters will pass by soon. I'll use Eaters. It's a super-risky, idiotic idea, especially with Grey Wolf around, and knowing they all go when one goes into a frenzy. The Eaters are coming from everywhere. I jump in front of the next passing Eater.

Just my luck; this Eater is huge. He gives chase. He isn't as fast as most. I run back down the alley toward the guards. Right before I reach the street, I jump in the air and grab hold of the fire exit stairs. They creak and crack under my weight. The Eater runs under me, trying to catch my legs. With all my might, I kick the Eater on his shoulders, sending him into the street where the guards are.

One guard is peeing behind a crashed HUV. The Eater gets back to his feet. I expect him to turn around and run back to me. Something about the patrolman's pee sets the Eater off. He chases the guard instead. The guard doesn't even have time to pull up his pants. He runs and screams for his partner's help. He is peeing everywhere. His partner runs from behind the patrol HUV. He sees the Eater and takes aim, but his peeing partner is blocking the shot. The Eater chases after both of them now.

Here's my chance. I sprint across the alley and jump on the patrol HUV, taking two steps and then leaping as high as possible. My head and shoulder are over the top, and then my waist. I pull my knees to my chest and tuck my body to flip forward. When I do, Sophia slips from my shoulder. I do everything I can to catch her. No matter what happens, I have to keep her on this side of the fence. It will all be for nothing if I don't. I catch her, but the top of the fence sheers off a small piece of Sophia's stock. I land hard but have no time to think about it as I roll into the first crater. It's disgusting. I extinguish the flame on the butt of my rifle. I've seen nothing like that. The fence is electric, but the top is like a laser.

Dried-out eyes stare at me like they're wondering where I've been. Most of the Eaters have swelled up beyond normal proportion. If I had a knife and stabbed one, it would explode. Parts of their bodies are purple from where blood has built up and dried inside their bodies.

Don't let their teeth lacerate your skin, is my first thought. My second is, I wonder if the Grey Wolf saw me, because if he did, I know he's laughing at me right now, crawling on these bodies. Maybe it's part of his game.

Bang! A shot rings out from behind me. Not a sniper bang. More of a handheld pistol pop. If jumping over that fence didn't get the Grey Wolf's attention, that gunshot sure will. The two guards come running out from behind a small brick building. They are out of breath and keep looking over their shoulders. They run straight toward their HUV. I see why they are running so hard and fast now. About ten Eaters come around the corner, chasing them.

The HUV starts. I am twenty feet from the jets. I can feel the heat from the exhaust rush over me. The Eaters in the crater closest to the jets start to char. Like striking a match, the tops of their heads ignite in flames. I can't tell if the smell is a pleasant change—or worse. The HUV takes off at full throttle. All ten Eaters run head-on into the HUV. Most of them die. One is fried to death when it steps into the path of the afterburners. The few that survive the initial hit of the HUV stand and chase the vehicle down the road, all but one. He stands at the fence line, staring in my direction. He can't see me. There is no way he can see me in this pile. He must smell the regular, un-mutated humans in here. His eyes are black, like one large pupil, and he has no lips. His left cheek is hanging on by a thin layer of skin. It drapes over like a curtain, almost touching his shoulder. He's looking in my direction. Maybe the Eater sees me. He could give me away if he does. I crawl to the other side of the pile, keeping out of sight of the condo windows. I reach a spot with a better view of the apartment. I lay myself out, mimicking a dead body like I did before. Trying to get as comfortable as I can in this predicament I'm in. I secure Sophia and point her up at the condo windows. The Eater repositions himself. He's standing right behind me. Staring at me again. It's freaking me out now. I can't shoot the damn thing. I can't walk over and stab it. I'm hoping if the Grey Wolf is watching, he thinks this is standard for Eaters. I go back to looking up at the condos and ignoring the Eater.

An hour passes. The Eater stands there, staring at me the whole time. It knows the fence will electrocute him. He's got to be one of the smartest Eaters I've ever seen.

From the sixth floor, the Grey Wolf cannot identify a living person in the pile of so many dead bodies. Only if I move. It's the best camouflage I have right now. Just being human. No paint, mud, ferns, grass, or sticks. Just me.

Something is furtively touching my thigh. Whatever it is, it's persistent. I shake my leg to get it off. I'm in a pile of dead bodies, so it's probably an insect. It keeps trying to get through my pant leg. I'm curious because I'm in the middle of winter when bugs are absent. What could it be? Maybe an Eater is still alive and trying to bite me. I look down and see three fingers wiggling. They are extended straight out from under a tangled mess of arms and legs. I move away from the fingers and pull my buck knife out, ready to slice them off. With a closer look, I see one eye staring at me. I'm not sure why I look at this eye, but it looks glossy, moist, and profound in the pile of bodies. Then it does something the other eyes haven't done. It blinks. What the...? Is someone under the pile? I move limbs around and slide a few bodies off to the side. I keep my knife ready just in case it's a fresh Eater. The face is getting more familiar. The skin is pink, and the face has full lips. His eye squint when the sun hits him. It's a male. It's...

"Woody?"

I hurry my pace to free Woody.

In disbelief, I say, "Woody, how did you end up here?"

His lips are chapped, and he can barely speak from his dry throat. Scratches run across his face. It looks like someone used fingernails to separate his skin from his skull. He is bleeding from one of his ears. He looks rough. I hand him the water bottle Mac gave me. He drinks a few gulps and takes in a deep breath.

"Oh man, I couldn't breathe with all that weight on me."

"How the hell did you end up here?" I ask.

"When that old white-haired guy took Jaysi, I followed them here. In seconds of being here, a herd of Eaters started chasing me. I ran as fast as I could, but I rounded this corner and ran into a patrol HUV. Right into it."

Woody rubs his ear, where the blood trickles down.

"I bounced off the damn thing. Then, I went into panic mode and took off running. One Eater reached her hand out...her nails were so damn long. I got away and made it a few streets over before tripping over some Eaters that were missing half their bodies. There was like a mountain of 'em. They looked like something had gnawed on 'em. Then a huge HUV truck turned on its spotlight. I just dropped to the ground and played dead. It scooped me up with all those Eaters and dropped me off in here."

"Crazy!" is all I say.

"Yeah, crazy. Except…"

"Except what?" I ask.

Woody holds his arm up. His expression is grim. He points to a sizeable chunk of meat missing from his arm.

"You're bitten!"

"One of those damn Eaters was still alive. It was pitch black in the back of the HUV. It happened so fast. I felt its teeth sink right into my arm. I pulled it away, and this huge chunk came out when I did. I started kicking that area with the heel of my boot. I just kept kicking. Then the bottom of the HUV opened up, and a hundred dead bodies fell out."

I realize why that damn Eater is standing at the fence. It smells Woody's arm. Even in this pile of dead bodies, it smells the scent of that one bite.

Peeuwoooooo. I look up at the condos. The blast echoes off the walls behind me. It's a sniper rifle. That's a sound, I know. He's in the condo and won't likely shoot from there again. He'll change positions. I know he will because that's what I would do.

"We need to go, Woody."

Woody looks at me. "We? No, Drift. You! You better go. I'm a dead man."

I get in his face. "Can you still move? Can you still run?"

"Yeah. I still have muscle control. For now."

I grab his shoulder. "If you're willing, I have a plan."

I tell him that Jaysi is hanging from a crosswalk, and Number One, Mac, and Kyle are probably the reason for that fired shot we just heard. The Grey Wolf doesn't miss. Not usually. Knowing the Grey Wolf is in the condos and not at the hospital, I need to get to the exits and block them. He'll be on the move. This time, Woody doesn't hesitate to join me.

Woody and I run over to the charging station and climb to the top of it. There are three feet of separation between the station and the Exa-Bot. I look at Woody.

"Listen, we have to jump on the Exa-Bot and then over the fence. If you touch the top of the fence…"

"I get it. I'm dead," Woody says. "Even if I make it over the fence. I'm dead… I'm ready!"

Woody jumps from the charging station and onto the Exa-Bot. I follow right behind him. The second Woody lands on the Exa-Bot, it turns on. His weight sets off some alarm.

"Vandals! Vandals!" a computerized voice echoes from speakers on the Exa-Bot.

The Bot detaches from its charging station. Woody jumps and clears the fence just in time. When the Exa-Bot turns its hover thrusters on, I lose my footing. It pulls away from the fence. I get to my feet. I run from the front to the rear of the Exa-Bot and plant my right foot to get a strong lift. The Bot moves away from the fence. I leap from the back of the Exa-Bot and into the air, just making it over the fence. Woody doesn't have much longer before paralysis sets in. He knows it too.

21

We reach the entrance of the condo. The glass doors are gone. Broken in a million pieces. As we step off the sidewalk and inside the lobby, the glass crunches beneath our boots. I work my way deeper into the lobby. Soldiers or Ghost Villagers are here. I know it.

Woody spots a plush chair. It's torn and faded. He plops down in it with no cares at all. He sinks deep into it and leans back, putting his arms up on its armrests. I look at him and grin. I work my way to the elevators. I press the button, but it doesn't light up. I give it a second just in case it's still working. Nothing.

I work my way to the stairwell. The stairs are the only other exit to this place. Woody is keeping watch here so I will go up. He has to be on floor six or higher. That's where I would be. I open the stairwell door and walk inside. As I walk up the stairs, each step feels like an eternity. I reach level six, cracking the stairwell door.

Everything echoes. The building is entirely concrete inside. I slide out of the stairs without opening the door any farther. Making sure it doesn't slam, I hold the door until it closes. I walk down the hall slowly and cautious. Most of the doors are open, so I'm able to look inside the rooms. Each open door I look in, I can see Jaysi in the distance. There's a herd of Eaters under her now. From here, it's hard to see the hospital roofline. Floor six is a good place to start in an eleven-story building. I realize there are four rooms that have a line of sight to Jaysi. That will help in my search. It eliminates most of my options. This floor and floor seven are empty and clear. I walk up the stairwell.

Floor eight. Nothing.

Floor nine. Nothing.

Floor ten.

I walk three-fourths of the hallway. Up to that, it was empty. I stop in front of the fourth door from the stairwell because the door is closed. I grab the handle and turn it. It's locked. Of all the floors I've checked, this is the first locked door. I prepare myself for hand-to-hand combat. I get ready to kick it. I take two steps and lift my right foot. With all I can, I force it to the left of the handle. The door flies open. I gain my balance and lift Sophia to my shoulder. Upon entering the room, a blast of wind hits my face. It causes a vacuum in the room, and the door behind me slams shut. I fall to my stomach in a ready position. As soon as I do, a bullet hits the door behind me. I didn't hear any gunshot, just the sound of the bullet exploding into the door. It's a trap. The Grey Wolf is past the hospital building. I crawl back to the door. I extend my foot out to push the door with my boot. The vacuum from the wind makes it difficult to push. When it does open, a Red Empire soldier is standing in the hall. He looks down at me on the ground. Lifting his leg, he comes down with the heel of his boot. I roll away from it. When his heel hits the floor by my head, I grab it, throwing him off balance for a split second. While I have a hold of his right foot, I kick him on the side of his left kneecap. He doesn't fall, but he stumbles forward. He's holding a handgun and starts to turn it toward me. Sophia is lying across my body and not in shooting position. I don't have time to aim her and pull the trigger. All I have time to do is pick her up by the barrel and ram the butt plate in his throat. The loose skin of his neck curves inward and around the heel and toe of the butt plate. He flies back, discharging bullets from his handgun. The bullet hits the ceiling. Small bits of concrete fall to the floor. *I've got to get in the hallway and to my feet before he can shoot another round.* I roll into the hallway and stand up. I get Sophia in my grip. The grip I know so well. I point it at the soldier to kill him, but before I can, high-velocity debris flies into my face. The Grey Wolf shoots a second time. This bullet goes through the door next to my head, splintering the wood. I fall backward. The soldier in front of me tries to get his composure and take aim. I don't even take aim. From on my back, I hold Sophia at my hip and pull the trigger. The bullet goes into his chin and exits at the top of his skull. He flies backward, and his muscles tighten. Brain matter and blood remain on the ceiling. When he hits the floor, the gun fires one more time. This time, I have no idea where the bullet went. I just know it didn't go through me.

The Grey Wolf knows I'm here. For all he knows, I'm dead now. I start back down the stairs. I open the stairwell door to the lobby and find Woody armed with a fire extinguisher, ready to swing it at my head. Relief comes to his face when he realizes it's me.

"Did you kill him?" Woody asks.

"No. Not the Grey Wolf. It was a trap. The Wolf is set up past the hospital. He put a guard up there 'cause he knew I'd look up there. But, I did get you something," I said.

I threw him the gun that the soldier had.

"Oh, yeah!" he says as he looks at it.

We run to the parking garage again and start walking through it. This time is different. We aren't alone. Eaters emerge from the shadows. They smell Woody's bite. I point to the stairwell.

"If we go back, we won't be able to get to the hospital," I say.

Woody doesn't hesitate.

"You run to the stairwell. I'll go back to the condo. The Eaters want me, not you."

It's hard not to argue with Woody. If he wasn't bit, I would have said no. But we are running out of time, and so is he. I just nod. He takes off running and so do I, in the opposite direction. I make it to the stairwell and run down two flights of stairs. I don't even stop to see if it is all clear. I swing the door open and run to the same alley I was in earlier. Halfway to the hospital, I notice a hundred Eaters under Jaysi now. It's terrifying seeing her like this. She looks passed out from here. I weave in and out of fallen HUVs and alleys. I reach the emergency room entrance. The Grey Wolf's cargo HUV is parked by the doors. I slow my speed and walk to the doors. They slide open. *Power?* It has to be part of the game. The waiting room is empty and too large.

Upon entering, I see a large, crescent-shaped desk. It has to be the welcoming desk or the nurse's station. I look over the counter, making sure nothing is hiding behind it. Papers are scattered everywhere. On the wall behind the counter is a dry-erase board. It has an "on duty / off duty" column with red magnets sticking on the board. All the nurses' jobs for the day are next to their names. The last things they did on their last day of work. It reads:

Betty – blood pressure, shots & pills
Linda – bedpans & sponge
Rebecca – desk & phones

The rest of it is smeared. I come to a fire exit sign. It has all the emergency exit routes on it. I study it. It also says the crosswalk is on the twelfth floor.

I told Mac and Number One to meet me on floor ten if they couldn't get to Jaysi. Since Jaysi is still dangling from the walkway, they might be there waiting. I get to the elevator doors. Before I press the up arrow, I look at the stairwell. *I'm too tired to climb stairs again,* so I press the button. To my amazement, it lights up, and a few seconds later I hear a ding. The doors slide open with grace. No one is inside so I walk in. This building must be on the same grid as the one running the electrical fence.

I ride the elevator to the tenth floor. When the doors open, I stick my head out and back into the elevator. No one is there. I exit the elevator. A few fluorescent bulbs flash above my head. With so many windows the floor is well lit. I work my way around the corner and come to a hallway. There are rooms on both sides of the hall. Cautiously, I walk the hall going in and out of each room. Halfway through checking the rooms, I enter one and stop. On the other side of the window, I see the rope. It's right in front of me. I walk to the window, and there she is below me. Her head is facing down. The wind is whipping her hair back and forth. She looks lifeless. She's been hanging there for at least an hour. I want to bang on this glass and give her hope. I want to let her know I'm here. It takes everything inside me not to.

"I want to break the glass too," a voice says from behind me.

I turn, aiming my gun in its direction. Number One is sitting on the floor with his back against the wall. A puddle of blood has formed under him.

"One? Oh, man."

It's not like me to not look in a room before I enter it. Then again, it's not like me to think of someone night and day either. Jaysi has all my thoughts. Number One grunts in pain, which brings my attention back to him.

"What happened?" I ask as I take a knee beside him.

"I...I couldn't stand seeing Jaysi hanging like that. I tried breaking the glass a few floors down, but it just wouldn't break. I hit it with everything. It just wouldn't break. She looked at me. She could see me. When the glass wouldn't break, I ran up to the crosswalk. I made it out to her. I had my hands on the rope. I pulled her up a foot or two and then I heard it."

"The gun shot?" I ask.

"No, the thud. I heard the bullet hit me long before the gunshot."

I inspect the wound. He has gauze under his shirt. It's soaked through with blood. The bandage is no longer absorbing it.

I stand and walk around the room, looking for more gauze.

"In the drawer." Number One points to a white dresser across the room.

It must be where he got the first batch. I grab one of the packages and rip it open, pulling out the clean white cloth.

"Let's change this out," I tell him as I remove the old gauze. I toss it to the ground. It is so weighted with blood that it made a loud splat. I hand him the clean gauze, and he applies it over a hole just below his liver. Damn, I thought. That's not okay.

"The Grey Wolf stationed a soldier in the condo. I think that's who shot you, not the Grey Wolf. He knew the condo would be the first place I'd look. I think the Grey Wolf positioned himself over here somewhere. Somebody was shooting at me from this direction while I was in the condo."

"I heard shots coming from the roof," Number One says.

Number One puts his hand on the sterile white linoleum floor to stand. Once he's on his feet, I notice his handprint on the floor. It's the perfect outline of his bloody fingers and palm. I can't help but think of the dry-erase board for some reason. The last historical details of his life are on the floor of this hospital now.

Number One is leaning on me at this point. Riding up to the twelfth floor, I see myself in the silver doors of the elevator. A view I see little. My face is dirty, and my jacket is even worse. I can't help but wonder what Jaysi saw in me if anything at all.

Ding!

The elevator stops, and the doors open. I ensure the area is secure, then give Number One the all-clear signal. He walks off the elevator and sits down. I investigate the floor just in case there are any surprises. I go in each room. A few skeletons lie in some of the hospital beds. Why bother? That's what I imagine these patients saying to their doctors.

There is a lot of equipment in these particular rooms. More than normal. It seems like the floor you died on. The dying floor.

As I go from room to room, I notice a reflection in the window from the other building. The outline of a head peeking over the roofline. I initially thought it was the Grey Wolf, but the hair is too dark. He is on top of the building. I watch the reflection until I hear the crosswalk door open. I hear Number One screaming out.

"Jaysi, we are here. Jaysi!"

The head in the reflection disappears. I run back to the crosswalk door. Number One is standing out on the crosswalk, pulling on the rope. How is he doing this? In my head, I play out what would happen if she made it all the way up. I'd have to run out there and untie her fast. The Grey Wolf wants that. It's part of his game.

Number One keeps pulling and pulling as hard as he can. Massive amounts of blood are coming from his shirt. He is doing it. He is lifting Jaysi. If I run out there to help, I'm dead. I sit at the door, holding it open with the toe of my boot. I push the door open until I hear a locking mechanism click. I stay in the recesses of the corridor, hidden from any unwelcome bullets. The Grey Wolf would love to have another person poke their head out.

"What are you doing?" I yell.

"What…ever…it…takes." He strains to get Jaysi higher and higher. "Stay there, Drift. I'm already dead. Just stay there."

Bang! Bang!

Two gunshots ring out. Close shots from a handgun, not a rifle. I wait for Number One to topple over the rail, but he keeps lifting. Out of nowhere, a Red Empire soldier falls from the roof. I ready Sophia. My first thought is the Grey Wolf shot him so he could kill us himself. I aim my rifle toward the shots. When I do, a head of blond hair peaks over the roofline.

"Woody!" I yell. I am so happy to see him. My smile is visible. He gives me a big smile back. He points to the gun.

"This is way better than an ax." He points down. "Kyle is on floor ten. I'm coming down to help you guys."

He was supposed to stay at the condo. The fact he isn't paralyzed yet is amazing. My first thought was to hunt for some antibiotics for Woody until something caught my eye in the door's reflection. The door is almost mirror-like. I can see everything behind me outside. I can see the entire mountain range and the tree line. It's crystal-clear too. A sudden flash comes from the tree line. I know who it is, and I know what it is. The longest shot I've ever seen.

"Woo…." Before I can finish Woody's full name, his head flies back. He falls backward. Woody is dead. The Eaters didn't get him. A bullet did. It's a matter of seconds before Number One takes the next bullet. I look at Number One and notice he's making a lot of headway in pulling Jaysi up. He has made so much progress he has tied the excess rope around his waist. He stops pulling once the knot is tied and lies on his back. He looks like he is in agony out there. Now the rope runs from the rail to his waist and down to Jaysi. I can't figure out what he is doing.

"Knife! Throw me your knife!" he yells.

My hand drops to the sheath on my right side, where my knife was strapped. I pull it out and slide it over. The butt of the knife hits his leg. Reaching out his rope-burnt hand, he grabs the knife. He sits up and begins slicing below the knot steadily until he has cut through the rope. Once it is done, he looks at me.

"You're gonna need this." He sets the knife on the ground. He doesn't slide it to me. His hands are too full.

"What are you doing?" I yell.

"Saving Jaysi."

He pushes to his feet, muscles straining from the effort, lifting Jaysi with him. His feet drag across the silver metal with a slow shuffle toward the rail. I know what he's about to do. He will use the rail like a pulley and him as the counterweight. Before he can leap, I spot another flash of light reflecting off the door. No gunshot noise this time, only the thud of a bullet striking Number One in the back. I count out loud: One, one thousand. Two, one thousand.

The bullet had only two seconds of flight time. The blow threw Number One forward, but he kept his footing. He continues, determined not to let anything stop him from completing his mission. Upon reaching the rail, he leans against it and glances back at me with a slight smirk before toppling over. Blood smears onto the aluminum as he falls forward.

The rope rushes over the metal railing, producing a sound like a zipper. As Number One goes down, Jaysi comes up. Her body jolts when it slams against the rail. I hear a thud followed by a loud moan from Number One. Number One hangs where Jaysi once was. His bullet wounds drip blood, putting the Eaters in a feeding frenzy.

The door opens on the other side of the crosswalk. It is Mac and Kyle. Mac sees me sitting on the floor and does the same, pushing the door back with his foot.

"Now what?" he yells.

"Can you see the tree line in the reflection of that door?"

"Yes," he answers.

"Grey Wolf is in that tree line. The tallest tree to the left. Near the middle. You see it?"

"Yes," he says.

"Look for a yellow flash. The second you see it, tell me! Ok?"

"Ok," he says.

"Tell me quick and fast!" I yell.

I stand and take a few steps back. Then I take off, racing down the hallway. Once I get close enough, I slide on my knees and grab the blade from the floor. As I kneel near Jaysi, I start sawing away at the rope.

"Flash!"

He didn't even finish with the "s" and "h." I move to the side. The bullet hits the railing close to Jaysi's hands. I keep sawing at the rope. I grasp Jaysi tightly before I slice the last of the rope. With it being so taut, the blade cuts through it quickly. Jaysi drops forward in my arms. My peripheral vision catches sight of Number One falling to the ground. I avert my eyes so I don't have to witness him landing below. When he makes contact with the road, I hear his bones collapse.

"Flash!"

I instantly roll myself and Jaysi over.

Thwack! I don't know what the bullet hit, but it sounded like it ricocheted off metal. I grab Jaysi's arms, pulling her to the crosswalk door that I left propped open.

"Flash!"

I dive with all my strength. Keeping hold of Jaysi, I fall through the crosswalk door. The bullet goes through the propped open door, creating a spider web with a two-inch hole in the middle. Inside and safe now, I lift her to a sitting position. She leans up against the wall and pulls her knees to her chest. It must feel good to bend them. I lift my water bottle so she can get some fluids in her. She puts her hands on the bottom of the bottle to help me tilt it to her mouth. When she does, I see the rope burns on her wrists. They'll heal over time, I think to myself, but there will always be the two scars: the emotional and the visible.

"Stay here. I've got to get Kyle and Mac."

Before I can walk off, she grabs my hand. "Thank you!"

I don't know how to answer her. I lean forward and kiss the top of her forehead. An odd reaction for me, but it feels right.

"Number One is the one to thank, but I'll explain later."

We walk back to the propped door. Kyle is still sitting there, and Mac is behind him.

"Come across," I yell.

"Are you crazy?" Mac says.

"Get a running start. He doesn't even know you guys are there."

"Are you sure?" Kyle says.

"Absolutely. Do it one at a time," I reply.

I take up position a few feet back in the building. Being in an ideal spot, I sit down, lifting my knee, resting Sophia on my leg. It feels great to have her close again. From here, the tree line stands out sharply against everything else.

"Here I come." I hear Kyle's nervous voice. In my readied position, I take a deep breath. I slowly exhale, trying to calm my racing heart. My finger rests on the trigger as I pause. No complex scope or dials to adjust, just pure accuracy with this shot. The wind whistles as it passes through the hospital's exterior, like a tornado rumbling down a street. Navigating the wind will be difficult. This task won't be successful, but I want the Grey Wolf to understand that we know his whereabouts. I'll need to be fast, faster than what was anticipated. Kyle will run in front of me when he passes the crosswalk. I may shoot him if he moves more quickly than I predict.

Kyle runs. I can tell from the vast strides of his boots on the metal grate floor. When I see the flash, I readjust my aim. I move Sophia one inch to the left. I shoot. As soon as the bullet leaves my rifle, Kyle crosses in front of me. A split second sooner, and he would have been limping the rest of his life. Kyle breathes heavily when he comes to a stop. He slouches over and puts his hands on his knees to catch his breath. He looks at me from his hunched-over position.

"Did…did you just use me as bait?" Kyle asks.

"No, I just thought it would be easier if you were here. And I figured if you were going to run across, I might as well take a shot."

"Did you get him?" Kyle asks.

"That's the problem. I can't just walk down there and check. I don't think I did."

"I'm ready," Mac yells.

I doubt I got him. Sophia is pointing at the spot the flash came from, just in case he shoots again.

"Come on," I yell back at Mac.

His footsteps on the crosswalk aren't as loud as Kyle's, but I know they are coming. Mac passes in front of me. No muzzle flash from the Grey Wolf's rifle, but I still know I didn't hit him. There's no way. He's just on the move, that's all. Like we should be.

"He didn't shoot. Maybe you got him," Mac says.

"Don't count on it, Mac. He's just moving positions."

We all walk over to Jaysi. She smiles at the sight of our faces. She's beyond happy to see us. I rummage through the closets and find many medical supplies, including bottles of antibiotics and ointment. I stuff everything in my pack. When I return, I put the cream on Jaysi's wrist, rubbing it on slowly and easily.

"The Eaters are in a frenzy down below. We should get out of here."

Inside the elevator, I see myself in the silver doors again. This time, it's Jaysi leaning on me. I think this is how I want to see myself for the rest of my life: holding Jaysi.

23

The elevator stops at the second floor. I figure it's safer to get off here just in case a few straggling Eaters are lurking on the first floor. Leaving everybody hidden in a room, I go down and scout out the first floor. With Jaysi so weak, it's better this way. After inspecting the floor for twenty minutes, I return to get them.

"Is everybody ready?" I ask.

There are no voices, just nodding of the heads.

"Ok. Follow me," I say.

We make our way down the stairs, but before my foot hits the first floor, the sound of the automatic sliding door grinds open. I lift my hand to tell everyone to stop. With caution, I creep around the corner and catch sight of two Eaters. After they pass the threshold, the automatic doors slide closed. Their hauntingly sluggish movements seem all too familiar, as if they are searching for something—or someone. They wander past the half-crescent desk where the work-board is. Eventually, they disappear into the hall's darkness. Thinking the worst is over, I take a deep breath. All that relief disappears when I look out past the closed automatic doors. Countless numbers of undead monsters are outside.

"We're surrounded by Eaters. I'm not sure how to get out of here."

"Maybe there's a fire exit?" Mac says.

Mac and I start to search, but I am quickly distracted by a group of Eaters who have moved toward the buildings across the street. They arranged themselves in neat rows, standing close together as if they were hiding from something. Every one of them walked up to the wall and leaned against it before starting to sway back and forth in unison.

"That's what they did in the library," Mac says.

"Beast! Eaters must be able to smell the Beast or something. They're afraid of them," I say in a soft tone.

"So am I," Kyle says.

Luckily, this side of the street is clear except for the two Eaters in the hospital with us. If we try to run down the street, the Beast will pick up our scent. Jaysi is too weak to run anyway, but we can't stay here. Right outside of the sliding doors, parked on the street, is the Grey Wolf's cargo HUV. It's the only idea I have.

"We could get in that cargo HUV and see if it starts," I say with not a lot of enthusiasm.

"How do you know it'll fly?" Kyle says.

"I don't, but it's the same one that was at the library and Ghost Village. It's got to be the Grey Wolf's."

"Can you drive it?" Kyle asks.

I muster up a little confidence. "Yeah...I can. Mac and I will get the HUV, come back, and get you guys. If something happens to us, go back to the second floor and find a different route," I say.

Mac and I make our way through the lobby. We approach the sliding door with caution. I notice a push door beside the sliding door. We go through that instead of having the sliding door noise alert the Eaters that we are exiting the hospital. Metal pillars are holding up the immense ceiling of the emergency room drop-off area. We work our way in and out of the pillars. Mac hides behind a valet parking podium for a split second. As soon as we get close enough to the HUV, I slide open the driver's side door and climb in. Mac jumps in the cargo bay. This HUV is used to transport Beasts. You could smell the pungent predator stench when we got in.

"Shit!" Mac said.

"What's wrong?"

"Shit! There's shit, everywhere. That's what's wrong," Mac yelled.

Before Mac closes the double doors or I can close my driver's side door, we hear an enormous roar that makes my stomach drop. I quickly shut the door and watch Mac through a small window separating the operator's cab from the cargo area.

"Did you hear that?" Mac asks, muffled.

"Hang on, Mac." I take my eyes off Mac in the mirror to look down at all the controls, only to realize it is in another language. I'm used to maybe five buttons—tops. This one has no less than fifty.

"This isn't like the old ones I drove, Mac. There are more gadgets than I'm used to, and it's in Russian."

"Just press a button. Any button!"

I press a large red button I spot near the steering wheel. The instant I do, the cargo bay quickly slopes backward like a dump truck. Mac has no way to stop himself from sliding to the back of the truck, and when I hear a loud thud, I know he must have crashed into the double doors at the end.

"Owww! Wrong button! Try another one."

I press it again. The cargo bay starts to level back out, and Mac becomes visible again in the rearview.

"Sorry."

Mac runs back up to the window to see if he can offer some assistance. Through the small opening I can smell Mac is covered in the stench. I press another button. The window dividing Mac and I turns to a cloudy frost.

"Damn it," I say.

"I can't see you. Press that button again," Mac screams.

I press the button again, but this time, a retractable metal door slides over the glass. I press it another time, and the metal door retracts, and Mac's face is visible again. For the first time, it has an unpleasant look on it.

"That one!" Mac pounds his fist against the window, desperately pointing at two buttons high on the dash and side-by-side. His hand thuds against the glass repeatedly until I put my fingers over the buttons. He nods at me with an eager thumbs-up sign, his face radiating intense anticipation.

"Yes. Yes," Mac says excitedly. "Left engine, right engine. You need to press both at the same time," Mac explains.

"How do you know?"

"I just feel it," he says.

I jab both buttons with my finger, sending an electric jolt of energy through the HUV. The engine's deep rumble intensifies and lurches off the ground, flying several feet into the air. All the lights in the cockpit flash to life, including a bright light in the cargo bay that illuminates Mac like a spotlight. The roar of power blasts under the seat, and I can feel it rattling my bones.

"We gotta go, Drift. Whatever is making that noise sounds pissed."

I gun the HUV forward and smash into a pillar—sending a deafening, metallic screech through the air. If that Beast didn't know we were here before, he sure does now. Struggling to keep the HUV below the ceiling, I back it up toward the sliding doors. The glass doors open. Jaysi hobbles as fast as she can to the passenger side and climbs in. Mac opens the back doors, and Kyle jumps in the back with him. When Mac closes the back doors, the two Eaters from inside the hospital run out. The doors close, and one Eater hits the back door with a thud. I push the controls forward, jetting us out from under the ceiling. Glancing into the rearview mirror, I think I see one of them keeping up—until Mac laughs hysterically.

"This Eater's shirtsleeve is caught in the back door. Go faster."

Before I can hit the thrusters a sudden impact whips us sideways, slamming my head into the driver side window with a sickening thud. Kyle and Mac are thrown mercilessly against the cargo box, denting it outward with their body weight. The HUV careens through the air, crosses the street, and plows straight into a horde of Eaters, wiping them out.

"What was that?" Jaysi screams.

"It's a damn monster," Mac yells.

It's a Beast, but this one is different. It's bigger and stronger than the last three. Maybe this one is a male Beast.

I slam the thrusters forward, cutting through a horde of Eaters in our desperate attempt to get higher altitude. The HUV is heavier than usual, making it difficult to move fast. As we slowly gain speed, I see the Beast, its eyes focused on the HUV. With one powerful lunge, it grabs hold of the Eater caught in the door and whips its head from side to side with a savage roar, shredding it apart before spitting out its mangled remains.

It lunges forward again with a single-minded purpose: kill us. Its head is right outside of my window. I can see its razor-sharp teeth glistening blood from the Eater it ripped apart. Our eyes lock for a split second. Then its broad shoulder pounds against my door, sending us careening off course as I wrestle against the vehicle's weight, fighting for control. It crashes into the side of a building, throwing brick and mortar everywhere.

Instead of a nice, slow, gradual turn, we take an immediate right, rushing back across the street and through the glass entrance of a clothing store. The HUV crashes through empty racks. The Beast stays behind us the whole time. It leaps into the air and lands on top of us. The weight causes the HUV to sink a few feet. I slam the afterburners in reverse. The Beast rockets off the HUV and directly into a wall of mirrors, sending an explosion of light through the air as shards of glass splash onto the ground. I launch us into reverse, with the hologram on the dash popping alive with a 3D image of our surroundings; arrows pointing me in every direction, warning me what lies ahead. Through the front windshield, I glance to see the Beast racing toward us, its powerful muscles rippling beneath its hide. Its entire body quivers in rage.

I bite my lip as I attempt the tricky maneuver of flying in reverse, careening around checkout counters and dressing rooms before finally bursting out of the store. The daylight causes me to squint. I jerk the HUV and spin it around. I slam the thrusters, and an intense boom erupts like a sonic explosion. Before we can build momentum, the Beast rams us again. It causes the HUV to hit the storefront brick. I keep the thruster at full force. We gain velocity as the Beast keeps pace behind us for a few blocks before disappearing in my rearview mirror.

"Main fly zone or follow the tracks?" I scream to Mac and Kyle.

"Whatever is closest? Just get us out of here," Mac replies.

We're closer to the fly zone at this point, so I turn on the up ramp. When I do, a patrol HUV comes in behind us. I never slow the thruster. We speed ahead, not bothering to look back until a barrage of fifty-caliber bullets screams by us. I throw the car into a wild series of zigzags. The tracer rounds rip through the air with a fierce intensity that I can almost feel burning my skin.

"Faster," Kyle screams.

"This is it. The thrusters are all the way!"

I look in the mirror, but there is no sign of the patrol HUV.

"Jaysi, find the reverse hologram. I need to know where this guy is," I say.

Jaysi frantically presses buttons, her fingernails turning whiter with the nervous press of each push. The radio roars to life, and electric guitars thrash through the speakers in cadence with a bass line that sucks the air out of our chests. Again, she stabs at the buttons. Suddenly a hologram pops out from the dash showing what's behind us.

"You did it," I say excitedly.

"Finally!" she says.

Jaysi sticks her fist inside the hologram and slowly opens it. The hologram starts to zoom in on the patrol HUV behind us. I can see the silhouette of the driver. She opens her fist more and zooms in closer. And there he is—an old Asian man with white hair at the wheel, illuminated in all his glory by the artificial light of the hologram. My heart races as I ask Jaysi, "Is that him?"

After a long pause, Jaysi answers, "Yes. That's him."

Jaysi is having trouble breathing as she looks at his digital hologram face. His cold visage sends shivers down my spine. Jaysi gazes transfixed, unable to break away from his stare until she finally closes her fist and extracts her hand, causing the hologram to zoom out. The view from our HUV is one of death and destruction: miles of lifeless HUVs.

Still not getting the altitude we need, the cargo HUV grazes across the rooftop of a dead machine below. The metal grating causes Jaysi to jump. "Higher!" Kyle screams.

I yank the two levers next to the thrusters. Pushing down makes it go up, and pushing up makes it go down. My brain wants to do the complete opposite. The HUV lifts a little. We get a good enough distance between the HUVs on the ground and us. Looking at the hologram, the patrol HUV is no longer behind us. Suddenly, *thump, thump, thump!* Tracer bullets pierce the roof of the cargo bay, zipping past Mac's and Kyle's heads, creating small beams of daylight. The patrol HUV is above us, shooting down. I veer left to throw off their aim.

"Damn!" I say in disbelief.

"What? What?" Kyle cries desperately.

"It's back!"

The Beast is moving quickly, crushing the roofs of the abandoned HUVs with each step. Even in the hologram, the Beast looks enormous. The patrol HUV above us is keeping a steady pace.

"I have an idea," I said.

I pull back on one thruster and forward on the other spinning us around. The patrol HUV zips by and spins around too. The cargo HUV is pointed right at the Beast. I slam both thrusters. The HUV starts to vibrate as we build momentum. The patrol HUV is directly behind us, and the Beast is in the windshield.

"You're gonna play chicken?" Mac says.

"We won't survive if you hit that thing head-on," Kyle says.

I grab my seatbelt and fasten it as I tell Jaysi to do the same. She stares at me, wide-eyed, with terror on her face. I reach up and rest my hand on the up/down lever. The Beast is getting bigger as it's rapidly approaching. It launches itself in the air, lunging at us. Its timing is perfect for landing on our hood. In the last second before impact, I push back on the lever, and our HUV falls to the ground. Mac and Kyle are thrown into the air and smashed into the roof. We have a split second of zero gravity before they come down with a loud thud. The bottom of our HUV screeches as the metal scrapes against the ground. The Beast soars over the windshield and the cargo box. It didn't calculate me dropping out of the sky. I glance at the rear-view hologram and see it smashing through the front window of The Grey Wolf's patrol HUV with an explosion of glass and metal.

"Yes!" I scream.

I don't have time to revel. Looking out the front windshield, I see a dump HUV standing tall out in front of me. I quickly wrench down the lever to gain altitude, but our HUV is sluggish. Our heads jolt as we contact the dump truck's top. An earsplitting scraping against steel screeches out—the holograph is now over-loaded with sparks.

I look backward to see if the Grey Wolf is still in pursuit, but the hologram turns pitch black. Suddenly, our necks jolt forward again, and Kyle and Mac slam into the divider window with a loud thud. I hear a crunching sound as the Grey Wolf's patrol vehicle hits the back of our cargo HUV. The force of the collision causes our rear end to drop and the nose to lift in the air. Before I can regain control, our thrusters slam into an abandoned HUV on the ground, causing us to flip head over heels. The Grey Wolf's patrol vehicle hits us mid-flip, sending us crashing hard onto other aban-doned vehicles. In an instant, we are amongst the grounded vehi-cles, bulldozing through the wreckage, tossing them aside like toys, paving a trail of destruction in our wake. We slide for at least thirty yards before finally coming to rest between two burnt-out HUVs. Around me, metal is twisted beyond recognition, and debris litter is everywhere. I have no time to assess my injuries or even note the ringing in my ears as the Grey Wolf's patrol vehicle closes in on us.

I quickly unfasten my seatbelt and Jaysi's. She is unconscious.

"You're the worst driver ever!" Kyle says rubbing his head.

"Whatever you do, don't open that back door. I need to see if the Wolf is dead."

The rear hologram is distorted, occasionally flickering off and on. I grab Sophia and make sure she's loaded. My window is right next to one of the old grounded HUVs. I crawl out of the window and lean against the charred cargo HUV. Dust and ash fall like snow landing on my jacket.

Peering around the corner of the HUV, I get a glimpse of the Beast. It's still wedged into the window, but there is no sign of the Grey Wolf. We were too busy crashing to notice the Grey Wolf crashed too. I race from HUV to HUV, military-style, my rifle ready. When I reach his patrol HUV, no one is inside. A pool of blood is dripping from the Beast onto the seat. Looking closer, I see the Grey Wolf's rifle—barrel bent and useless. He left it behind. I lift my head back up to scan the perimeter for any sign of him. When I do, I notice Jaysi stumbling toward me in the middle of the road, her head bleeding from the crash. She appears to be dazed and confused. As I dash forward to help her, a sudden gunshot splits the air, and a bullet narrowly misses me as it slams into the ground near Jaysi's feet. Panic floods me, and I scan desperately for any sign of what direction the bullet came from. I know it wasn't a sniper shot.

My feet pound the ground as I run, desperately trying to reach Jaysi before it's too late. But the grounded HUVs are in my way, blocking my path. With no other option, I jump onto their roofs and leap from one vehicle to the next. Another shot rings out as I take another step to jump to the next HUV. A bullet strikes near my right foot. The metal ting is centimeters from my boot. Adrenaline races through me as I land on the next HUV, determined to reach Jaysi before any more shots come our way.

The Grey Wolf doesn't miss, but he's already missed twice now. There is no time to think about why. With no time to spare, I leap into the air, my arms stretching desperately to reach her. Another shot is fired. As I clasp my arms around her, a burning sensation takes over my right bicep as we fall to the ground. I check Jaysi for any wounds. She is clear.

I open the closest abandoned HUV and shove her inside it. She falls on the laps of two skeletons. I figure she is safe in there. Shutting the door, I feel a trickle of blood down my arm. I've been shot! But I am more concerned about saving Jaysi than feeling the pain. Fortunately, it was me who took the bullet instead of her.

Keeping my footsteps light, I make my way toward the shots, being cautious not to draw attention to myself. I'm sure he's changed position, but I have to start somewhere. My adrenaline wants to hurry but each step is a slow and careful. The Grey Wolf is among this wreckage. As I pass a flipped HUV, I feel a deep slice across my shin, cutting it wide open. Stunned, I fall to the ground, and my head strikes the surface before I reach out and break my fall. The Grey Wolf rolls out the window, thrusting a knife at me, but I roll out of its way in time. We both get to our feet. The Grey Wolf's hair has streaks of blood dripping down it. I reach for Sophia, but she isn't there. She came off my shoulder when I rolled.

He lifts his right hand. He has a pistol in it. The gun is shaking and unsteady. His face grimaces. When I look closer, I see his index finger and his middle finger are missing. Blood is streaming down his forearm. A sniper's worst nightmare. His trembling hand seems to shake more violently the higher the pistol goes. He struggles to steady his aim. With lightning speed, I push the gun away and spin around, striking him with an elbow to the face. The gun soars across the wrecked HUV and slides to the ground on the other side. He stumbles backward. I can't take my eyes off his menacing glare.

He lifts his right hand and slowly tucks his blood-soaked hair behind his ear like my blow did not affect him. I see the white of the bone poking through the ragged flesh where his fingers had been—the Beast must have gotten one last bite in. We lock gazes.

"I have dreamt of killing you. Not like this, though. In my dreams, you're in my crosshairs, and my first bullet strikes you right in the chest. Right here." The Grey Wolf points to his heart and taps it a few times with the point of his knife. "Then, as you fall to your knees, you look in my direction, gasping for air. Your lungs filling with blood, suffocating you. Then I squeeze the trigger and send another bullet."

The Grey Wolf taps his forehead with the tip of his knife giving an evil smirk. "It hits right between the eyes, and my name—my name is on your lips as you fall to the ground. But how lucky am I? I get the chance of seeing you die, close-up."

The Grey Wolf roundhouse-kicks me square on my jaw. I would have been knocked out if it was a few inches lower, followed by my throat being slit.

The momentum of the fall puts me on the hood of a HUV. With no time to spare, he follows his roundhouse kick with a cross punch, landing his right palm above my right ear. My ear starts to ring. He pulls his hand back faster than he threw it, grunting in pain. He winces, grabbing his hand for a second but lets it go. I can tell he doesn't want to show any signs of weakness. His bloody nub left a thin layer of his blood on my face. I wipe it off. He thrusts the knife at me, but I hurry back, making him miss. He tries again, but this time he swings it instead of thrusting. I tilt my head back a few inches. The tip of the blade soars an inch from my eyelashes. With his balance off, I throw a punch and land it squarely in his rib cage. He swings the knife back at me, but I grab his wrist. With one hand holding his wrist, I throw multiple blows to his rib cage with the other. My thumb digs deep into the tendons below his palm. I'm able to manipulate his wrist and cause him to drop his knife. I am so focused that I do not see his knee until it was too late. A solid hit to the groin causes me to let go. He swings with his left hand. I see it coming and tighten my stomach muscles. He lands a direct blow to my stomach.

It's my turn to make a move. I throw two quick punches at him. He dodges the first one, but the second one lands on his beak. He stumbles back a few steps, and I see his eyes tear up, showing that it was an effective blow. Before he has time to recover his vision, I jump on the bumper of a HUV and lunge forward, hitting him squarely on the cheekbone. He recoils and hunches over in pain. My hand throbs, but I don't have time to check it; instead, I lift my leg and come down hard with my boot heel right onto the back of his skull. The Grey Wolf drops to the ground beneath me. As I lower my foot to finish him, another blade slices through my calf. The Grey Wolf has found a knife.

This time, I don't fall. I step back, limiting the chance of another gash. The Grey Wolf gets to his feet, holding the knife tightly. I know he's right-handed. With his injuries, he's out of balance. He won't have the strength he normally does. His left hand is not as coordinated as his right. This could be my opportunity.

The Wolf rushes toward me, his knife pointed straight at me. I step aside, swinging my left forearm down and hitting him between the bicep and forearm. His elbow bends upward. I grab his hand that is wielding the knife and bend it back. I thrust my weight forward. The blade slides into the Wolf's throat as if it belongs there. He looks at me, wide-eyed. With his hands hanging limply by his sides, blood gushes from the wound, coloring his lips crimson and running down his chin like fresh red ink on his pale white face. Before he collapses to the ground, he utters a faint "Drift" through struggling breaths.

The Grey Wolf lands forward on his stomach. The butt of the knife caused his neck to twist.

With two of their HUVs destroyed and one of their best soldiers missing, the Red Empire would soon arrive to investigate. I start pacing around, looking for Sophia. Dropping to my hands and knees, I find her resting under a HUV. I clutch her tightly as I struggle back to where Jaysi was and notice she has already unlocked the door and is sitting on the ground outside.

"Did you really put me in there with two dead bodies? Are you out of your mind? You know how awful it smells in there!"

"I… I'm sorry. You were so disoriented. I didn't know what else to do."

Jaysi rose from the ground, looking at all the blood.

"Are you okay?" she asks. "Oh my God. You're shot."

"My legs are cut up pretty bad, too."

My knees begin to shake, and my words slur. My vision starts to blur, and red dots chase one another when I shut my eyes. My legs can't handle my body's weight any longer and give out. The fall to the ground feels like it takes an eternity. When I finally land, I feel nothing. A lack of blood has weakened me and left me exposed and exhausted. My last image is Jaysi collapsing to her knees beside me, then nothing.

Heat. All I can feel is heat; it's like I have entered hell. As things began to come into focus, I realize I am in cabin one. The blurred lines of the room turn into visible shapes. I see the smiling family staring back at me in a picture on the nightstand. My eyes struggle but focus a little farther out. Along the walls are shelves lined with books and journals neatly arranged alphabetically—I am in Jaysi's room.

My attempt to sit up is painful as my head and shoulder throb from an injury. The bandage on my shoulder is bloodstained and taped haphazardly. Thirsty beyond belief, my lips are dry and cracked, and my throat feels raw. When I dangle my legs off the bed, I can feel the cuts on my shins throb and my slices jiggle.

The gauze strips on my leg are cleaner than the ones secured to my shoulder. They must have opened my pack and got everything I took from the hospital and used it on me. As I carefully remove them, I discover what has been causing that uneasy jiggling sensation throughout my body. My skin is covered in stitches—it looks like a patchwork quilt made from flesh and meat. The sight of the wounds immediately sends itches racing throughout my body. I grit my teeth and clench my fists, trying not to scratch them.

It's a struggle, but I cautiously stand. I slide my feet across the hardwood floor. I'm afraid that taking solid steps might cause the stitches to come out. I shudder at the thought of being awake while someone puts new ones in. After all, someone put a lot of effort into threading these.

The cabin is empty, so I carefully walk down the hall to the living room. Someone has gone out of their way to make sure this place is clean. As I get to the living room, I hear voices from outside. I open the front door and am temporarily blinded by the light that streams in. After my eyes adjust, I see a Ghost Villager pass in front of me. My heart sinks. I frantically start looking for a weapon to defend myself when I recognize Mac's voice.

"Drift! Drift's awake," he says. His voice stirs the villagers into a commotion. All the busybodies stop in their tracks and put their eyes on me. Isabella and Kyle walk out of the barn. Mac wipes brown grease off his hands with a dirty rag as he walks toward me. He walks up the steps and hugs me. The pain is sharp but soon dulls.

"Glad to see you up and moving," he says.

As he lets go, he puts his hands on my shoulder and gives me a good shake. Again, I feel all the stitches on my body jiggle. I let out a small grunt.

"Oh, sorry man. I'm just happy to see you up and on your feet," Mac says. The clang of tools and banging of wood grabs my attention. I watch as fifteen folks from both Ghost Village and Hill Top work together on cabin two, side by side.

"What's happening?" I say.

Mac looks at the cabin with me. "Oh yeah. Man. Our neighbors came to help us rebuild. You've been out for three days. Lot's changed."

"I see that," I say.

It looks like the barn has become the center of activity in the village. There's a constant stream of people coming and going. The cabins belonging to Connor and Woody have been consumed by flames, but I can still hear their axes ringing out from within the barn walls. It seems someone else has taken their places as woodsmen.

Isabella and Kyle stare at me from the barn. Isabella pecks Kyle on the lips. I understand what Mac meant by a lot has changed. Kyle and Isabella start walking toward Mac and me. When they get to us, we walk back into the cabin. Mac puts his arm around my neck.

"I took the liberty of packing your stuff and putting it in Jaysi's room. Jaysi was kind enough to trade beds with ya. She wanted you to be comfortable."

"Where is she?" I ask.

"Last I saw her, she went to get some water. She's been taking care of you the whole time. But she's not the same, Drift. I think that whole thing downtown messed her up."

I have no response. I can only imagine what Jaysi went through and what she's living with now. All the people I killed in war still follow me around. I can see all their faces clear as day still. All of them. Mac doesn't take long to bring it up.

"Well, you put in your time. The Ghost Villagers brought back that box of ammo we promised you too. It's in the barn where Jaysi's been sleeping. Are you going to stay with us?"

"I don't know, Mac. I just woke up from being out for three days. It'll take months for this to heal, but I know there's not much wide-open space in a room with four walls. I can't stand the heat in here."

"It's not the walls, Drift. You can walk outside at any time and see wide-open spaces. It's all about who you share the walls with," Mac answers.

"Yeah, I guess, but people die when I get comfortable. People I love."

Mac puts his hand on my shoulder.

"We all die…Why not spend your living days with the people you love? That's what living is, isn't it?"

I don't know how to react. I smile and put my head down. It does get lonely in the woods by myself. There's no denying that.

"I know I'll need to heal up a little more. That'll give me time to think about it," I say.

Mac smiles and answers fast. "Perfect."

"Jaysi's been talking about archiving your story," Mac says.

"I don't know about that," I say.

"Honestly, I think she just wants to know who you were. Before all of this. Sounds like she might have a thing for you," Isabella says.

They're my stories. Stories that make me look and sound like a monster.

"I don't want you to think of me that way. I'm no hero," I say.

"You're a hero to us," Mac says.

I notice Isabella looking at my dry, cracked lips.

"Oh, Drift! You're starving. Let me get you some soup." She walks outside and back to the barn. In minutes I'm sitting at the farm table, surrounded by friends, eating soup. It's amazing.

With the shrinkage of my stomach, I eat a little bit. I want to see Jaysi. I want her to know I'm awake. I want her to know how thankful I am for her stitching me up. There she is. She is walking up the path next to the barn. She is holding a bucket of water. Some water splashes out of the bucket and onto her pant leg. One of the Ghost Villagers approaches her, and I can't help how my spine stiffens. The Ghost Villager takes the bucket of water and points in our direction. I relax a little. Jaysi looks up at the cabin. She doesn't see me. She nods at the Ghost Villager, turns, and walks into the barn.

The hour is getting late. The sun is sinking over the barn, and still no sign of Jaysi. I can't stand it anymore. I put my swollen foot into my boot. My foot is tight, even with my laces as loose as they can be. When I stand to walk out, I pause. My heartbeat pulses in my foot and around my stitches. It takes a second to get used to the throbbing. I limp onto the porch and stop, but still no Jaysi. I head to the barn, passing a few smiling villagers.

The barn Is dark and drafty. Mac sees me walk in. He walks to the two new kids chopping wood. I don't know what he tells them, but all three walk out of the barn. I walk to my old stall. Jaysi is lying on my old bed, reading.

"What are you reading?"

I startle her. "What are you doing out of bed? You need to be resting," she says.

"I can't rest anymore," I say.

She looks at her book and then back at me.

"Harry Potter," she says.

"Who's that?" I ask.

"Not a who. Well, it is a who, but it's the book I'm reading. I found a whole box set in the cabin when we first found this place. It's full of adventure and bravery. It takes me to a different place when I read it. Everything here disappears when I read it," Jaysi explains.

"Is that why you're in here? You want to be at a different place?" I ask.

Jaysi doesn't answer. She shuts the book and sets it down. I can tell something is different.

"Is everything ok?" I ask.

"Yeah, why wouldn't it be?"

"You didn't come to the cabin and see me. I was hoping you—"

"I'd what? Come running, thanking you for saving me, and then kiss you all over," she says with a little tremble in her voice.

"I was thinking more—Drift you're up! Glad to see you're doing ok. Now get out of my bed and move back to the barn where you belong. I don't know…something."

Jaysi stands. "I'll move back to my room."

"Ok. I'll get my stuff." I turn to walk back to the cabin. When I look back, Jaysi is gathering her stuff.

It is more confirmation that things have changed. Mac was right. I know what she is going through. I've been there. Surrounded by so much death changes a person. Before I walk out of the barn, I turn to her again.

"It's not your fault, you know," I say.

"What?" she asks.

"Number Two's death. Woody's death. Connor's death. None are your fault."

"I never said they were," she responds.

"I've been where you are. I can tell you blame yourself. That's how my heart hardened too. It's not your fault. The Red Empire, the Eaters, and the Grey Wolf are the reason. You had no say in it."

Jaysi looks down at her feet. Everything she was holding drops. She puts her hands over her face and starts to weep.

I'm not sure how to react. I move to hold her, but she shrugs me away. I return to the cabin and grab my things with Mac's help. I carry them to the barn. Jaysi isn't there. Her stuff is still where she dropped it. Mac and I pick it up, and Mac puts it all back in her room at the cabin. Later that night, Jaysi returns to the barn to sleep. Her eyes roll when she sees me where she should be sleeping.

"What are you doing here?" she asks.

"I told you I'd move back out here," I say.

"I was being sarcastic, Drift. I'll sleep here until you're better."

"Mac took all your stuff back to the cabin already. I always feel more comfortable out here, anyway," I say.

"Fine." Jaysi turns to walk out of the barn. I hurry to my feet and rush to her. I put my hand on her shoulder. She stops walking.

"I don't want it to be like this, Jaysi. I'm not sure what I've done," I say.

"You haven't done anything."

"Maybe that's the problem," I say. "I haven't done anything."

Jaysi turns around. She never looks me in the eye. I swear, killing is easier than this. I can't move right now. I want to say a million things, but I can't think of the first thing to say. With no words coming to mind, I do it. I lean in and kiss her right on her puffy, soft lips. She accepts the kiss for a second and then pushes me back.

"You need to teach me how to fight, how to shoot. I won't be a victim anymore," she says.

"Are you sure?" I answer.

Jaysi lifts the right sleeve of her jacket to reveal the rope burns around her wrist.

"No more! No more friends dying just to protect me!"

I want to tell her, *I know how you feel,* but I keep my mouth shut. She knows how I feel. I've been telling her and the whole village why I stay far away from people and like being alone.

"I'll teach you," I tell her. She looks me in the eye, then stands on her toes to kiss me. This kiss lasts more than a second. It's an eternity, or so it seems.

Weeks pass, and I find myself hunting again. It feels good to walk through the woods. Instead of shooting Sophia, I set up snares. My shoulder can't handle the recoil right now. I'd hate to go through all the rehabilitation again. A few rabbits in the trip wire and a squirrel or two keep the meat steady. Jaysi has been coming with me. She carries Sophia and takes practice shots every day. Her aim is getting better, even without the scope.

I haven't seen any patrol HUVs since the death of the Grey Wolf. It's peaceful and quiet. Spring is here. I can tell by the thawing of the creek, the chirping birds, and the flowering trees.

After hunting and hand-to-hand combat training every morning, Jaysi and I return to the cabin for breakfast. We sit across from each other, and, after we eat, she pulls out her pencil and writes in her journal. Archiving my story. I don't know what good will come of it, but it's something Jaysi wants, so I do it. I'm tired of fighting it.

My stories don't surprise her. Bullets cracking skulls and exploding eyes are the norm now. Even the description of a knife carving through human skin no longer affects her. Today is a good day. I am done with my stories. I'm at the beginning of where my life starts here. She recorded my last day of school, the last day I saw my mom, the first day of basic training, how I met Sophia, and how I was the last surviving soldier of my unit. Now that the archiving is finished, Jaysi and I will visit Ghost Village tomorrow. We were asked if they would like to merge villages and become one. Kyle thinks we would be stronger if we all lived in the same area instead of a day-and-a-half hike from each other.

The melting snow made the trail slushy. Even though my joints no longer hurt, I still cautiously navigate around rocks and roots on the path. Jaysi insisted on carrying Sophia for practice. She wants to get used to the weight. It's big on my shoulder, but on hers, it's as long as she is. Even with the strap tightened, the butt of Sophia almost touches the ground.

A few miles out from Ghost Village, a cloud of black smoke rises from the trees.

"Is that Ghost Village?" Jaysi asks.

"It is."

When I answer, a thunderous roar screams throughout the woods. A Striker Drone rockets across the treetops. It's heading in the direction of Hill Top. When it passes, the treetops sway from the wind.

"Should we get back to Hill Top?" Jaysi ask.

"We're closer to Ghost Village. We should check on them."

We pick up the pace. I can tell I'm out of shape. I haven't been hiking long distances since my stitches came out.

Knowing the perimeter of Ghost Village, I have us come in from the mountainside. It puts us at eye level with Striker Drones and out of reach of patrol HUV guns.

We duck behind a large rock, almost on the verge of tumbling down the side of the mountain. From this spot, I take in what is left of the Ghost Village below. At least forty Red Empire soldiers are visible. All the houses and cages are set ablaze. Although the smoke is clouding my vision, I can still make out two cargo HUVs parked side by side. One has its bay doors closed while the other is being loaded with the Ghost Villagers. I pray it's not a Beast in that extra cargo HUV. Jaysi looks up at me, her face twisted in fear.

"What should we do?"

"Nothing. Not against so many of them. We need to get back to Hill Top," I say.

We hunch over and scuttle away from our position, making a beeline for Hill Top. Hopefully, we'll make it there in time.

25

The cold night air slows our steps, so we take breaks to eat the snacks Isabella made for us. The chill makes my injuries and scars throb, but eventually, the sun rises between the trees. As we return to the trail, its warmth caresses our faces as we step in and out of the shade of the branches. The aroma of burning wood grows stronger. Soon enough, the daylight is overcome by the smoke that hangs heavy in the sky. We are at Hill Top.

"We're too late!" Jaysi says.

"Shhh. Soldiers could be anywhere."

To keep our distance from the Hill Top, we go to the hunting grounds first. Jaysi and I are familiar with this area. Jaysi knows about reconnaissance now. She is aware that emotions get you killed out here. Running into the village, screaming and fighting, will not end well for anyone. We move to a better vantage point. The barn and cabin have been reduced to a pile of ash. Smoke still rises from the destroyed structures. There are two patrol HUVs parked between their former sites. A few soldiers wander the village while the cargo HUV and patrol HUV take off with plumes of smoke in tow. At the sight of it all, Jaysi gets tears in her eyes.

"All for nothing!" she says.

I ask her, "What?"

"All the archiving, for nothing! Mac, Kyle, and Isabella are dead, for nothing."

"We don't know if they're dead. Maybe they took them—"

CRACK!

Jaysi and I stop talking. It doesn't even have to be said. She knows to be quiet. We lie down on our stomachs, making our bodies small. We are calm and still. The ground is damp from the morning dew. I can feel my pant legs soaking up every ounce of it. Neither one of us is wearing our hunting camouflage. A good soldier will be able to see us. Jaysi maneuvers Sophia into a shooting position. She puts the butt of the rifle against her shoulder. Her index finger is scratching the trigger. I motion to her to hand me Sophia. She shakes her head no. I don't even try to take it because more movement would give us away. Plus, the shoulder strap is wound tight around her forearm. She's ready, I tell myself. This is why we've been training. A distant voice comes through the trees. Someone is walking the trail we use to get water. After a few moments, I spot them: one soldier in the lead, followed by Isabella and two other worn-down veterans. Isabella's hair is disheveled. Her face is red and battered as if she has been crying. I turn to Jaysi and hold up three fingers, and she nods in agreement. In hushed tones, I tell her, "We have to be careful; if we fire any shots, more soldiers will come."

Jaysi nods her head once more. Time is running out; they'll catch us if we don't act soon. I tap on the ground, signaling to her that she should shoot. But, still, no shot comes from Sophia. Suddenly, one of the soldiers notices our presence. His eyes widen in surprise, and he points toward us, alerting the other two by Isabella's side. Once more, tapping the ground with emphasis, begging her to take a shot. Jaysi doesn't pull the trigger.

"Come out!" the last soldier yells. "Come out and we won't kill you."

My first thought is, why aren't they shooting at us? Then I start to think. They've raided hundreds of villages, and no one's had rifles or guns. They don't know we have a sniper rifle aimed at their foreheads. The last soldier steps up and puts his gun against Isabella's head.

"Come out, or I kill her."

I look over at Jaysi. Tears streaming from her right eye, she confidently pulls the trigger of Sophia. The bullet careens through the forehead of the last soldier standing. His head snaps back with the force of impact, followed by his body falling. The gun he'd been pointing at Isabella falls to the ground. Then, the soldier behind her lifts his rifle and shoots in our direction. Jaysi quickly reloads Sophia and fires another round. The bullet pierces the soldier's chest, and he falls to the ground with a yelp. He clasps his hands over his heart as he collapses. He isn't dead yet, but he will be soon enough. The youngest kid stands there motionless, wetting himself. Jaysi reloads Sophia when a barrel appears from behind her—a gun unlike any we've seen before. On the other end is a soldier wearing an unfamiliar uniform. His rifle is advanced, like a sniper rifle but better than Sophia's. His uniform is black and sleek, making him look tactical and elite. Several pouches, straps, and other items crisscross the soldier's chest. A long, slender sword tucked in a sheath hangs from his back. On each arm, knives sit and wait to be used. Three others are standing behind him with their rifles pointed in our direction. He stops pointing the gun at Jaysi's head and takes Sophia from her, passing it to one soldier behind him. A soldier frisks Jaysi for any more weapons. Then it's my turn.

The new kid picks up his gun. He walks behind Isabella, pushing and shoving her. When they get to us, the soldier with the sword sees the piss-soaked pants. For a second, I think he will be sympathetic because this kid is clearly the new guy. He unsheathes his sword. He swings it left to right, slicing the new kid's throat. It all happened as fast as I could blink. The new kid drops to his knees. He falls to his right, headless.

Isabella screams. Jaysi is emotionless, and I'm confused. Why would he kill one of his own? The soldiers push us toward the patrol HUVs. The smoke burns my eyes. As we round the corner of the patrol HUV, I see the back of a leather chair. It's a nice chair too—black-leather-type chair CEOs use. Someone is sitting in the seat. The elite soldier holding Sophia shows her to the man in the chair.

It swivels in our direction, but the man's face is down. A hat covers his eyes. He's turning the pages of a book. Not just any book: one of Jaysi's. It's my archives. The man laughs. It's terrifying. He looks up, revealing his deformed face. It looks like someone smashed it with a rock. His left cheekbone is completely missing.

The skin below his eye socket is caved in. He stands and takes a few steps toward us, looking at Jaysi.

"Drift. I never knew your real name. I never knew you were a girl."

No one says anything. He walks closer to Jaysi and sticks his face in front of hers.

"Do you remember this face?" he asks. "No! Why would you? Especially now! The last time you saw this face was probably through your scope when you put a bullet through it."

The general put his finger into his concaved cheek. He walks around Jaysi.

"You are nothing like I imagined," he says as he runs his fingers through her hair.

I went to say something, but he turns and looked me in the eyes before I could.

"Recognize me yet, Drift?" he says.

He holds Jaysi's archive journal up in the air and shakes it.

"Best nonfiction book I've ever read. I believe I even made the cut. What's my name, Drift? Remember me yet?" the general asks.

I vaguely remember who he is, but I didn't want to give him the pleasure of knowing he did look familiar.

"I've had so many high-ranking officers in my scope. I have no clue who you are," I say.

His name is Liu. I remember him now. He was a tyrant, not a general. He raped and pillaged and held no respect for prisoners of war. Before I put that bullet through his cheekbone, I watched him torch a house with ten people locked inside. I remember that day like I do all my kills. Before I pulled the trigger, he was laughing. As people were screaming in the burning building, he just laughed. He laughed so hard his head tilted back as I pulled the trigger. I had the lines of my scope aimed right between his eyes. The wind was strong that day. I could tell because the smoke coming off the building swirled fast. Between the wind and him tilting his head, I must have missed the kill shot.

"You will get to know who I am soon enough, Drift," Liu says.

26

Two military personnel restrain me, Jaysi, and Isabella with zip ties and thrust us in the back of a patrol Hovering Utility Vehicle—HUV. Jaysi sits beside me, while Isabella and one soldier sit across from us. The vehicle rumbles as it takes off, leaving the ground below us with a lifting thrust. The gravity pushes our bodies back into the seat. A beam of light shines in from the rear window as we soar away, watching the mountains get smaller and smaller.

"I'm sorry," Jaysi says.

"It's not your fault," I reply.

An hour goes by. White clouds swirl behind the HUV. The power of the engine slows as we descend from the clouds. Through the window a city appears. Other HUVs zip past us. Below, buildings have replaced the trees I am used to.

The HUV alights on a grand landing pad. The cargo bay hisses as it decompresses. The thrusters drop to a low hum as they shut down. Daylight slowly creeps across the cargo bay floor as the back door lowers. We squint as we leave the patrol HUV, and a woman's voice is amplified through a bullhorn. She addresses a crowd of Red Empire civilians gathered on the rooftop.

"Ladies and gentlemen, the great Drift Allen and his team."

Some stare at us; others point and laugh. Three groups of impeccably dressed tourists, each led by a lady holding a pole with vibrant triangle flags of different colors—bright yellow, baby blue, and red. The crowd eagerly takes our photos.

The last soldier steps out of the patrol HUV and holds up my sniper rifle, Sophia. The crowd erupts in cheer and lifts their phones to capture the moment. After a minute or two, the woman holding the pole says something and walks toward the door. It was too muffled to understand. As the citizens all turn to follow her gaze, my spirits drop, and I understand that we are nothing but a show for the Red Empire. They want to parade us around for their entertainment.

Looking out from the landing pad, I notice we are in New York City, high above the other buildings. My stomach turns. In the mountains, I might be high in the air, but my feet are on solid ground. In a building like this, I rely on the people who built it. The wind is strong. It muffles noises as it blows by. Even if I tried to escape, where would I go? There are no tree lines to run to.

The sliding hangar bay door opens with a mechanical hum, bringing the scent of burning fuel, strange foods, and a faint hint of ozone. I've been so long in the woods that I've forgotten what it was like being in a bustling city. The sounds of far-off machinery, HUVs, and people's footsteps echo inside my head, pounding at my eardrums like a dog whistle to a K9. My quiet mountains are all but gone.

The marble walls and floors inside the hangar remind me of the library we visited long ago.

Then we move into a grand and opulent chamber adorned with lavish, golden-trimmed walls, and a magnificent sight unfolds before me. A resplendent Red Empire banner, regal and immense, unfurls from the lofty ceiling, its crimson hue commanding attention and exuding an air of authority.

Positioned before this emblem of power is a meticulously craft-ed desk, standing proudly as a symbol of order and efficiency. Three pristine young women grace the desk with their presence. Their ra-ven-black tresses cascade like shimmering waterfalls over their shoul-ders, harmonizing beautifully with their striking scarlet dresses. Their ears are adorned with sleek, inconspicuous earpieces, an indication of their crucial role as intermediaries between the Empire and its visitors.

With hushed voices that barely disturb the solemnity of the chamber, the receptionists interact with hologram screens, their fingers dancing quickly across the interface. The glowing projec-tions respond to their gentle touches, illuminating their faces.

As we pass the desk, all three of them pause long enough to give us a scrutinizing gaze. Then, the guards take us through a bustling area filled with people. All of them look at us as if we are outcasts. The guards push us toward a set of elevators.

Are they keeping Mac and Kyle here?

DING!

The elevator doors peel back slowly. Three civilian employees are inside, each wearing a badge with their pictures. They scurry off the elevator the moment they see us, and we walk in and take their places. There are others who were waiting for this same elevator, but no one steps on to join us.

One of our guards presses the button on the panel. The descent is quiet. No one says a word.

When the door opens, we are marched down hallways lined with soft carpet; I haven't seen such pristine beauty in a long time. Most of the carpets I'd come across were moldy and smelt of urine. Suddenly, we stop at the door. It swings open, and the guards push Jaysi and Isabella inside a room before swiftly shutting it again.

"Drift!" Jaysi screams behind the door.

I fight my way toward Jaysi's muffled voice, but the guards hold me back. I manage to get one hand free. Throwing a right hook,

I hit one guard in his ear and pop it good. He grabs the side of his head. Goodbye, ear drum. With the same free arm, I force an elbow backward and land it squarely on the second guard's chest. He takes a quick step back to keep from falling. Grabbing the doorknob, I twist it.

I hear Jaysi's voice.

"Drift!"

"I'm here," I yell.

I feel two needles pierce the skin of my neck. All muscles tighten. My legs give out. The buzz of electricity surrounds me as I fall to the floor.

Two guards stand over me.

"He wrecked my ear drum."

I cannot move, but I do feel the toe of his boot sink deep into my ribs, twice. I gasp. Air leaves my lungs. They grab my arms and lift my limp body off the ground. I can't lift my head. My feet drag behind me, leaving two lines in the carpet. I study the flower print on the floor. The pattern starts over every five steps the soldiers take. After four pattern restarts, we stop in front of a door. They heave me inside, throwing me on a bed—which is surprisingly clean and soft.

"Shower! Clothes! One hour!" One guard says as he points to the bathroom, then a closet, and then a digital clock. He speaks in short sentences. They walk out the door and leave me in the room alone. I can't move. My body aches. But, after a few minutes, I regain the use of my muscles. I look through the room for any means of escape. I draw back the curtains. HUVs zip by, one after another. There are buildings beyond number, and bright three-dimensional billboards line the HUV lanes. I turn from the window and look over the room. Two bottles of water and one cellophane-wrapped fruit basket sit on a table.

I shower, dry off, and open the closet door. An off-white outfit hangs inside. When I take it off its hangar, it feels weighted. It's not the kind of material I would want to wear in the woods or in wet weather. I put it on. The top is too big and the pant legs too short. I'm a prisoner now. Is this an outfit the prisoners of the Red Empire wear?

I glance at the digital clock. The door opens—exactly one hour since my arrival. Four guards are standing in the hallway.

"Let's go," one of them says.

We go down the hall, two guards in front and two behind, and I study the carpet patterns again. After four repetitions, I look up to see which room might be Jaysi and Isabella's, but I can't tell which one is which.

The elevator is waiting for us at the end of the long corridor. We step in, and this time, the guard hits the thirtieth floor.

DING!

The doors slide open. One guard shoves me from behind, forcing me off the elevator. I almost fall face-first, but I catch my footing. I look back and give him the death stare. I want to break his nose or pop his other ear drum, but instead I turn and walk forward. The room is enormous. Why am I here? Why did everyone hold their cameras up when I got off the HUV? My mind races.

The views are overwhelming. Windows run the entire length of the wall, and the incredible height makes my feet sweat. It's not like the mountains.

A man walks into the room, his tall frame towering as he sits at the desk. His angular face has prominent cheekbones and a sharp chin. The three-piece gray suit is perfectly pressed. The white shirt under his jacket is starched and crisp. The fiery red of his tie adds a splash of color to the otherwise austere appearance. He sits at the desk.

"I'm Mr. Hope," he says.

Two bodyguards stand like stone walls behind each of his shoulders. Their stares are hard and cold. They have on matching dark suits that blend into the room's background, like black holes absorbing light. Mr. Hope holds up Jaysi's journal. He runs his fingers over the smooth, black cover, feeling the worn edges where the material is rubbed thin. He stops at a gold vein that spells out the word 'journal,' and traces it with his index finger.

He looks at me with a broad grin and asks, "What secrets will this reveal? How many crimes will I find?"

"No crimes. I did what my commanding officer told me to do," I replied firmly.

Mr. Hope's brow furrows. His mouth turns to a frown as he sighs with disappointment.

"Well, that's no fun."

Then the corners of Mr. Hope's mouth twitch upward, stretching his skin into an unnatural crescent moon shape. The uncanny smile battles years of plastic surgery, nearly cracking the wax-like sheen of his face.

"I guess we'll find out sooner than later how true that is," he said.

He slips two fingers behind the cover and opens the journal. The handwriting is meticulous and elegant, with each letter formed carefully. He reads the title page out loud, and the four words resonate with a sense of solemnity: *I Alone: the Archives.*

Mr. Hope lifts his gaze from the page.

"Oh, my. How dramatic! And this handwriting, it's exquisite."

He presses his thumb and index finger briefly to his lips, lapping them with his tongue. Finally, he pinches the first page between his fingers and slowly turns it over. A deep breath leaves him.

My mind races. He is about to take in the details of my past. The history of who I was—or the beginning of who I am. I guess we'll see.

THE END

BOOK II

They filled the holding room with red plastic chairs, concave in shape like a person's backside. No one sat on them due to discomfort. On the video wall, holographic ads flickered and projected into the room to persuade us kids to part with our allowance credits. I suspected the school received a commission from ads when kids paid instantly with their phones.

This time, it was for some peppermint gum that came in bright green packaging. As its image spun in midair, a man with an enthusiastic voice spoke from the surround speakers.

"Caffeinated peppermint-flavored fluid explodes in your mouth with every bite."

A smell of peppermint filled the air. After the gum commercial finished, the next ad started. It was for a laser burn pen that could engrave names into wood or delicately etch words onto paper. With those things, kids could turn school desks into a wonderland.

A friend of mine strolled through the holographic 4D commercial. "What's up, boi?"

We gave each other a fist bump.

"Come on, Drift. We need those skills tonight. We gonna meet in the meta-lobby at seven."

"Man, mom wants to spend time together," I said.

"Bet, bet. Well, if ya get bored, power up. We gonna blast our way to the top," he said as he walks off.

Most of us hung by the edge of the ad wall, throwing our backpacks onto a pile near the exit, causing them to avalanche to the floor.

Fifteen minutes after school let out, my mom was stuck in the HUV line. Rather than being frustrated by the delay, I felt a slight thrill as it gave me extra time with my friends and more opportunities to impress Carlotta Caballes. She always caught my attention. I just never seemed to catch hers. Every time she passed, her skirt brushed against the edge of defiance, and her tan thighs disappeared into the shadows of mystery. All the boys would stop talking about meta-games and the new Fuel Force Eight. The teachers often said our generation lacked imagination, but we proved them all wrong when Carlotta passed by.

My go-to method for dealing with shyness toward girls was to crack jokes. The teacher who always was on duty for HUV pickup was the subject of my most memorable joke. Maybe he was getting extra credits for that job; why else would anyone take it? He had a mustache that looked like a walrus, so I took a black ink pen and drew a replica on my index finger. Then I took my inked finger, placed it on my upper lip, and wobbled around.

"Mr. Walrus, I presume," one girl said.

It got a few laughs. Our mascot was some deformed-looking lion, nothing like the other schools' digitally designed robot mascots. Instead, we had a hand-drawn MGM caricature rip-off of a yellow lion. The original picture was still in the principal's waiting room. An old photo of the artist holding an overly sized check for fifty dollars was next to it. It had to be a hundred-and-seventy-five years old. Since I spent a lot of time there, sitting in the red plastic chairs, I always wondered what life was like back then, with no HUVs or real-time gameplay in the meta. AI wasn't even around. People still did their own accounting I bet.

Parents abided by a strict policy for picking kids up with HUVs: they had to fly low and slow until they entered the school zone. Then, Autopilot mode would activate. It guided them up to the metal boarding deck and parked them level with the edge. It made stepping off the grated platform and into the car much more accessible. Unfortunately, the Autopilot wouldn't let them switch back to manual while in the school zone. Mom texted or took calls during this time since she didn't need to keep her hands on the wheel.

They announced my name through the speaker. "Drift Allan to the loading dock. Drift Allan."

I said goodbye to my friends and stole another glance at Carlotta, wishing for eye contact. With her head down, she looked back at me. That quick smile before she turned back to her friends was all I needed.

I walked out to the metal platform and waited. If I had known I wouldn't see my friends again, maybe my goodbye would have been more heartfelt.

I stopped at the bright yellow caution paint on the floor. It was thirty feet away from the actual loading zone. Once Mom hovered at a safe level, Mr. Walrus motioned it was ok, so I stepped past the caution paint. I could feel the rubber soles sinking into the teeth of the metal grate. I climbed into Mom's HUV, but before we took off.

Most kids took HUV buses. However, after I lost my father in World War III, Mom insisted she pick me up every day. She said she enjoyed the extra thirty minutes with me, but I think she was lonely.

"Hey baby, how was your day?" Mom began every conversation this way.

"Same ol' same," I answered.

"Now remember, I'm cooking dinner tonight. No running off with your friends. I want us to sit at the table and do that… normal family stuff."

"What? You mean you wanna argue back and forth?" I joked. "Then you tell me how my grades and social life suck while I ignore you and play on my GamePad? That kind of normal family stuff?"

"Hilarious! No, I want to hear about your day and what's on your mind," she said.

"Mom! I'm almost fifteen. What do you think is on my mind?"

"I don't know… Girls?"

"Girls!? No, Mom. Video Games."

"What about Carlotta?"

When the Autopilot steered us out of the school zone and released the speed controls back to Mom, she followed the slow-burn zone until we merged into the high-speed zone. We cruised for about ten minutes before congestion slowed the HUV. Unusual— the high-speed zone never had slow-downs. If there was a slowdown in the speed lane, it usually meant another HUV wasn't communicating with the mainframe. The central mainframe controlled all the HUVs and reduced traffic crashes by almost 95%, or so we were told. My whole life the HUVs had been on the mainframe, but I supposed there was a time you had to stop HUVs manually. Although you didn't have to steer the HUV, the law demanded that drivers kept both hands on the wheel just in case.

Every time our HUV passed over a business below, a commercial played on the passenger side dashboard since we were too high up to see their three-dimensional billboards. This one was for new high-end sports shoes. Initially, the hologram showed a spinning shoe and then it switched to a kid slam-dunking a basketball as if he could jump higher because of the shoes. I had the option to turn off the commercials, but they provided a distraction, so I didn't mind so much.

I pressed the radio display, searching for something to grab my attention when the screen flickered. Then a hologram of a cup of coffee with steam emanating from it appeared. It almost looked like it was real: lifelike and vivid. But before it completed its entire ad cycle, it dimmed and faded away. The radio screen went dark. Then, the hologram reappeared, showing the same cup of coffee. My search for something to listen to yielded only silence. The hum of the HUV was the only sound.

"Mom, did we pay the streaming fees?"

"I paid the credits for an entire year. I know I did," she said. "I bet they want us to update the software again."

The screen display flickers.

"Stupid streaming services," I said under my breath as the music returned through the speakers.

We were almost to the exit that took us to our world of suburban Nashville. My friends called it *the subs* for short. It was a program to help widows and widowers who lost their spouses during World War III. Thousands of these communities sprang up after the war. The government made the subs affordable by producing them at a low cost. In the winter, I could feel cold seep through the walls, and in summer, the air conditioner fought a losing battle with the heat. The water pressure was a slow drip. Outside, the noise came through the walls in stereo. I always wondered if architects ever considered the real people who would live there, but despite their faults, I loved *the subs*. They provided a comfort most neighborhood kids understood. We had all lost somebody we loved. When one of us got lonely or started missing our dads or moms, we could talk about it. Mom had a strong support group, too.

The HUV jerked to a halt. The seat belts dug into our shoulders, stopping us from going face-first into the dashboard. Suddenly, all power shut down. The lights faded away, and a deathly silence filled the cabin. But the HUV didn't just stop moving—a moment later, it dropped like an anchor. My stomach flipped as if I was on a roller coaster. I reached out to grip whatever I could find as we plummeted. There was a split second of zero gravity during the drop, causing everything to float around in my vision.

The weightlessness lasted until the engines returned to life, and the HUV climbed back to its normal altitude.

A moment of disbelief and dread hung there before Mom spoke, her voice calming me with a single sentence: "I'd better take us down."

Trembling, I uttered a weak agreement.

Then, before we could descend, all the dashboard lights went black again. The engine stalled, and my backpack and Mom's purse flew to the ceiling again. Mom's hair rose while we went down. Her scream made my ears ring. The engines failed to come back online this time.

When we hit the ground, we didn't bounce. The HUV's weight made sure of it. The impact was hard, and I felt every bone in my body shudder. Lucky for us, the seats had a hydraulic cushion for this purpose. When my teeth stopped clacking, and I could breathe again, I looked out the windshield to ensure we didn't hit another HUV on our way down.

But all the vehicles were falling from the sky.

"Mom, get out… Get OUT!" I screamed.

We opened the doors and scrambled to escape. Mom and I ran in opposite directions, and I glanced over my shoulder just as another HUV crashed down. The roof of our vehicle pancaked down to the afterburners with a thunderclap. Shards of glass blasted outward in all directions, slicing through the air. I raised my arm to protect myself, but it felt like millions of bees stinging me all at once. I tumbled onto my back. Mom rushed around the wreckage and lifted me up, her eyes full of fear.

"This way!" Mom cried.

She took off toward a nearby cafe. Someone inside flung the glass door open as we approached.

We both turned to look out the storefront window to see the gruesome scene of HUVs raining from the sky. In the distance, a commuter ship came into view. These HUVs were humongous and flew high in the stratosphere, able to travel great distances at high speeds. This one was careening through the clouds like a broken toy. The doomed commuter ship careened through the clouds in a vertical dive, and no thrusters could save it. The ship lost its momentum when it collided into a high rise, ripping it in half. Glass and steel rained down. It then hit the ground and bulldozed its way through building after building, decimating an entire block. Gray smoke saturated the air around the ship after an enormous explosion. The colossal blast sent more brick, mortar, and glass in all directions. The sky erupted with a big ball of red fire. Above the flame was billowing black smoke, swallowing the blue sky. I knew that commuter HUV. It was the one Carlotta's mom took for her daily commute from Nashville to London and back, reduced to a burning heap of debris.

"Jesus," I said under my breath.

Sharp beeps fill the cafe as an emergency broadcast emanated from every wall-mounted TV. The shaky footage showed battleships growing more prominent as they approached the shore. Hundreds of bullets hit the sand, tearing through sunbathers and families in a heartbeat. Screams of terror and anguish rip through the speakers. The white sand turns crimson as blood mingles with what used to be a peaceful paradise. Missiles tear through condos and surf shops.

A news anchor's voice penetrated the chaos.

"We are under attack. The Red Empire has invaded the shores of America. I repeat we are under attack. They have hacked our HUV mainframe, crippling all civilian transportation. Also hacked was the government's program, The Safety-First Security System, in the Gun Recognition Identification Department. The GRID has noted that all civilian guns are rendered useless. They can no longer shoot. Therefore, do not engage the enemy. I repeat, do not engage. They have rendered civilian firearms useless."

Another video plays. The footage is shakier than the opening shot. A man runs out of his house, lifting his civilian gun to shoot at the Red Empire ship. The gun doesn't fire. He looked at his weapon before throwing it to the ground. He tried to retreat into his house, but a bright flash appeared. After that, the video turned to static.

The original video loop started over.

We are at war. We are at war.

My mother's embrace was so tight it felt like she wanted to absorb me. We both stared out of the cafe window, watching in horror. Then an ear-splitting screech preceded the swarm of Striker Drones that flew past the cafe. Fear shot through me like electricity. Their uncanny accuracy decimated their defenseless targets. The drones sprayed the ruined HUVs with bullets, trying to cut down any remaining survivors.

There were no Red Empire soldiers and no HUV tanks. The battle was still a thousand miles away, but they programmed drones to hunt civilians, a scare tactic that did the job.

Moments later, the Striker Drones vanished without a trace, leaving us in the cafe for hours. After the shock wore off, my emotions got the best of me. I rested my head on my bent knees as tears started to fall. I did my best to hold them back, trying to be strong for Mom. She tickled my back to calm me down, something she used to do when I was younger. My friends' faces flashed before my eyes. Were they alive? Did they make it home before their school transport HUV dropped out of the sky? How could a kid like me protect my mom through another attack like this one? My chest felt tight, and my stomach tingled as it searched for hope.

Finally, the sun descended, and darkness fell. The owner offered cups of coffee, but Mom's trembling hands told me it wasn't because of the caffeine. Fear radiated from her body—I could feel it.

"We should go," Mom said.

"Now?"

"Yes, in the dark. We can make it."

I looked out the window. There was no sign of Striker Drones. "Ok."

Before standing, I wiped my face. Something in me didn't want the strangers in the cafe to see that I had been crying. But when I looked around, it seemed like everyone had been crying.

We walked to the door and paused.

"You can stay the night if you'd like," the owner said.

"Thank you, but we need to get home," Mom replied.

We stepped out of the place that kept us safe and began our journey home.

THANK YOU!

I am writing to express my heartfelt gratitude for your support and for choosing to read my novel. In a world filled with countless options, you took a chance on this book, and I am truly grateful for that. Not to mention that time is a precious commodity. I am humbled by the fact that you dedicated yours to delve into these pages.

I am excited to share that the journey doesn't end with this book. The second installment of this series, titled *I Alone Archives,* takes a unique twist as a prequel. This time, we explore the captivating journal of Jaysi, shedding light on Drift's origin. With a touch of whimsy, I crafted a fifty-thousand-word book to witness Drift's transformation from an innocent kid to a resilient survivor.

Your support really fuels my passion for storytelling. It's incredibly inspiring to me and makes me want to continue exploring this fascinating world and its characters. Thank you for the confidence to push the boundaries of imagination and deliver even more enthralling experiences in future installments. Readers like you make the writing process worthwhile and remind me why I fell in love with storytelling in the first place. Your support and encouragement mean the world to me, and I am grateful beyond measure.

ajbritt.com